"IF YOU VALUE YOUR LIFE, DO NOT MARRY ROLF CHEVAL."

What was meant by this horrible letter, and why was it delivered to me in Rolf's presence? I folded it, intending to slip it into my pocket, but Rolf stayed my hand.

"I cannot permit my fiancée to have secrets from me." His hand closed over mine. "As your future husband, I have every right to read that letter. Kindly hand it to me."

He seized me. A great pain shot through my arm and shoulder. The letter dropped to the table.

He frowned as he read the crude message.

"Who wrote this? By the devil, he shall rue it. Who was it? Some lovelorn suitor? If you think you can deceive me . . ."

BRIDE FOR A TIGER
was originally published by
Hurst & Blackett Ltd.

JO GERMANY

Bride for a Tiger

PUBLISHED BY POCKET BOOKS NEW YORK

BRIDE FOR A TIGER

Hurst & Blackett edition published 1973

POCKET BOOK edition published March, 1975

L

This POCKET BOOK edition includes every word contained in the original, higher-priced edition. It is printed from brand-new plates made from completely reset, clear, easy-to-read type. POCKET BOOK editions are published by POCKET BOOKS, a division of Simon & Schuster, Inc., 630 Fifth Avenue, New York, N.Y. 10020. Trademarks registered in the United States and other countries.

Standard Book Number: 671-77992-3.

Front cover illustration by Howard Rogers.

Printed in the U.S.A.

1

When I boarded the stage in London, I was ashamed of the out-moded calash I had inherited from Mama, and envious of the other ladies' feather trimmed bonnets. Now I was thankful for its warmth, for the north east wind cut through the cracks round the coach door and lashed about me and the only other passenger foolish enough to continue the journey.

Though I was wearing thick boots, my feet had long since lost all sense of feeling. Yet my fingers were warm enough inside the padded rabbit-skin muff, which old Daniel had made as a farewell present for me.

'You'll be as smart as any of them there court ladies with that to keep 'e warm,' he said, presenting it to me the day before my departure for the Hawkins' estate at Marshsea.

Dear, faithful, old Daniel. He had been my only true friend after Mama died. Three years later when Papa joined the navy, to help to protect England against Napoleon's threat of invasion, he had also become a cushion between me and my step-mother. More than anything, it was his guidance and advice I would miss in this new life which my maternal grandfather had so unexpectedly planned for me.

I eased my cramped limbs to a more comfortable position and looked at the snow piling on the window ledge. The journey had already taken a day longer than scheduled and my body was bruised from the constant jolts. If this was a sample of my new life, then I could well do without it.

At first the ride had been enjoyable. The sun had shone with a false promise of coming spring and the pretty hamlets and toll-gate halts provided pleasing diversions. The bustle of tavern yards as we stopped to take refreshment was something quite new to me. I delighted in sitting at a window table so I could watch ostlers exchanging tired horses for fresh teams; see friends greet each other and baggage being sorted. That night I slept soundly at the Little Rose Tavern in Cambridge.

Though my fellow passengers were surprised that a young lady of nineteen should be travelling alone on the public coach, the lack of a chaperone did not worry me unduly. I had long since been accustomed to fending for myself.

Yet, this was the first lengthy journey I could remember undertaking for I had been only two years old when Papa quarrelled with Grandpa and removed his wife and daughter from the Hawkins estate. A move which, perhaps more than anything, was responsible for Mama's early death. Having been reared as a lady of quality, she had not the stamina to withstand the rigours of life as a poor farmer's wife, which was the best Papa could offer after the rift.

Now, seventeen years later, I was being summoned back to Marshsea. Back to 'the devil's own corner of England' as Papa had called it.

I wondered if Grandpa had been worried by my non-arrival last night. There was no way of acquainting him with the news that the deteriorating weather had caused the coach to break an axle. Fortunately we had been near Littleport at the time and the landlord of the Globe had kindly sent his own coach to collect the stranded passengers. While we slept the axle was repaired and long before we had finished breakfast the coachman was urging us to hurry.

'The more miles we cover before the next snow storm the better,' he said, gazing at the belligerent, grey sky. 'The roads are well nigh impassable as it it.'

At first, progress was not too bad. Although the day was almost as murky as night, we reached King's Lynn before the first flakes flurried in the wind.

'It would be well to tarry the night here,' the coachman said. 'It be a wild road we travel next. Not fit for beast nor human a day like this, and no houses to offer shelter should we run into trouble. A proper haunt for robbers and footpads it is and no mistake.'

The majority of the passengers accepted his advice but, much though I wished to do so, I dared not, for fear of causing Grandpa further anxiety.

When we resumed our seats in the freezing coach I was alarmed to discover the only other person continuing the journey was my present taciturn companion. At first I was apprehensive of being confined in the carriage with him. Indeed, had the weather been fitting, I would have requested permission to travel on the high seat behind the driver, even though Grandpa had sent sufficient money for me to ride in comfort. However, none but a fool would choose an outside seat in this blizzard.

Yet my fears were quickly proved groundless, for the man paid not the slightest attention to me. Instead, he sat morosely huddled in his thick Garrick overcoat, with the top cape raised to protect his face and neck from the draught. His eyes were staring at the empty seat opposite, yet I was sure he was not seeing the leather upholstery. I wondered what thoughts could possibly be sufficiently unpleasant to bring such a deep frown to his high forehead.

I turned from him and rubbed the window, which our warm breath had clouded. Yesterday I had gained pleasure watching the skaters gliding like giant birds over the frozen rivers and dykes. Now the swirling snow blotted out all visibility.

I raised the collar of my green velvet coat higher about my neck and longed for the journey to end. A wheel rooled into a deep rut and I was thrown against the upholstery. I wondered what would happen if we overturned or broke a strap. Possibly we would be forced to accomplish the remainder of the treacherous journey on foot, or at best mounted on one of the horses.

The thought was alarming. I tried to obliterate it by concentrating on the future which awaited me at Marshsea, and in particular, upon the fiancé I had not yet met.

In his letter Grandpa had described Rolf Cheval as

wealthy and said that I should consider myself fortunate he had arranged such an admirable match for me.

'Fortunate indeed,' my step-mother said, upon hearing the news. 'If you want my opinion, it's long past time that old money-bag remembered his responsibilities, instead of leaving me with the burden of keeping you all these years.'

I was tempted to remind her that, far from being kept, I had worked hard for my bed and keep during the last seven years since Papa was killed at Trafalgar. Every morning I was up with the first light cooking, washing, feeding hens, milking the cow, churning butter and doing all the dozens of farm chores that needed attention during the hours of daylight. She would not easily find a replacement for me. Therefore I was puzzled by her eagerness to see me gone, until I remembered the way she constantly watched me whenever her new husband was at home.

Apart from being nearer my age than hers, Ben Tulley was well known about the village for his roving eye. Old Daniel first called my attention to my danger now Ben was living at the farmhouse.

'Always lock 'e door at night, lass,' Daniel said, 'and keep well clear o' that vermin. It be the farm he wanted, not the mistress. It takes nought above a fool to see that.'

As always Daniel was right. Ben made play for me one day when I was cleaning out the stables. Being forewarned I was ready for him and helped him outside with the aid of my pitchfork. I won that tussle, but I knew he would try again.

Now the problem of Ben Tulley was behind me. Although Grandpa's letter was phrased as a request for my return to Marshsea, it was in reality an order for, since my father's death, he was my legal guardian. A fact he had chosen to ignore until a few weeks ago.

I wondered why he had suddenly concerned himself about the future of a grandchild he did not know. Had he suggested the match or had Mr. Cheval? I wished he had told me more of my fiancé. Whether he was young or old; fat or thin. All I knew was that he was

8

wealthy. A fact confirmed by the beautiful sapphire and diamond engagement ring which a messenger had delivered at the farm three weeks ago, together with the money which Grandpa had sent for my travelling expenses.

So engrossed was I in my thoughts that the coach's increased speed went unnoticed until my hitherto silent companion said:

'What the devil's the fellow about? The coach will topple if he whips the horses to this foolish frenzy.'

With a brusque movement he stood up and slid down the window. Immediately the swirling snow speckled the coach's interior.

'Has the blizzard withered your senses,' he shouted to the driver. 'Stop this nonsense before you kill us all.'

Above the wind and jangle of horse brasses I heard the reply.

'I daresn't, sir. There be highwaymen behind, but have ye no fear, they'll not catch us if my name be Jake Wyatt.'

His whip cracked loudly over the straining rumps of the four snow covered horses.

My first thought was for my ring. Mr. Cheval would never forgive me if I allowed it to be stolen, yet where could I place it for safety. Certainly not in my pockets or reticule. I pulled it from my finger intending to push it down between the upholstery, then I realized that many another frightened lady must have done just that, as the robbers would well know.

My companion was having difficulty in holding his tall hat to his head, as he tried to peer through the gloom for sight of the men chasing us. His action gave me an idea. Quickly I took off my calash and tucked the ring into my chignon. No-one would think of looking there for it.

The coach lurched again and the man was forced to hold the window frame to retain his balance. I shuddered as the icy blast stung my face. Now it was possible to hear the shouts ordering us to stop. I had always imagined that I would be frightened if ever challenged by the so called 'gentlemen of the highway', but instead, my senses were tingling with excitement. A feeling encouraged by the knowledge that I had little for them to steal, apart from the ring which was now safely hidden in my hair. The brooch I wore on my coat, though prettily fashioned in the shape of a pansy, was made of painted tin and worthless to anyone other than myself.

The rogues were overtaking us fast. The muffled thud of their horses' hooves could be heard mingling with their shouts. I wished my companion would close the window. Leaning out like that was doing little good and I was becoming quite festooned with snow.

Now the voices were near enough to distinguish their words.

'Stop. Stop in the name of the law.'

'Who are you?' shouted my companion.

'Lieutenant Stubbs. North Norfolk Militia.'

'Do you hear that, driver?' my companion said. 'It's the law chasing us, not the lawless.'

I rubbed the window clear, but could see nothing through the gloom.

'How do we know?' asked the coachman.

'I can discern their uniforms.'

'If you say so, sir. The risk be on your own head. Whoa there, m' beauties.'

The horses, startled by the sudden reversal of orders, neighed their disapproval. As they slithered to a halt one of the riders appeared at the window.

'Your pardon for causing alarm, but our orders are to stop every vehicle travelling these roads, particularly all closed carriages.'

'The deuce they are.'

'As you may know, another batch of French prisoners of war has escaped from Norman's Cross.'

'Aye, it was all the talk at Wisbech and King's Lynn,' agreed my companion, 'but I fail to see how it concerns us. We're not responsible for their freedom. A stricter watch at the barracks would be more to the point.'

'I agree with you there, sir. If some of those prison officers were made to keep watch with us tonight, they'd be a deal stricter when they got back, I warrant. Trouble is, the worse the weather the better they like it, the damned frogs, I mean, it gives them a better chance of reaching the coast.'

'Well, Lieutenant, I can assure you there are no escaped prisoners in this coach. You can see for yourself, it contains only the young lady and me.'

He moved aside so the officer could look in.

'Good evening, Lieutenant,' I said, acknowledging his salute.

'Evening, ma'am. My most humble apologies for interrupting your journey. I trust it will not be long before you know the comfort of a blazing fire.'

'That is our desire too,' I replied, wishing he would be on his way, for the upholstery was rapidly becoming white with snow. But he was not to be hurried.

'Are you a stranger in these parts?' he asked.

'Yes.'

'May I inquire your name?'

My limbs were trembling with cold and I was losing patience with what I considered unnecessary questions.

'As I am neither a gentleman nor French, I cannot see the importance of my name.' I retorted.

'I have orders, ma'am. I must inquire the names of all strangers travelling these roads.'

My companion smiled at me and I was surprised to notice how pleasant his face could be when he was not frowning. 'I think it would be wise to tell the Lieutenant, so that we may be permitted to resume our journey.'

'Very well. I am Miss Henrietta Debnam.'

'And I, Mr. Howard Layton. Does that satisfy you, Lieutenant?'

'And your reason for travelling, sir?'

'That, Lieutenant, is entirely the concern of the young lady and myself. We have told you our names and that is all the information we are required to give.'

'I must know your destination, sir.'

The corners of Mr. Layton's mouth twitched as though he was trying to prevent a smile.

'As this road leads only to Marshsea and it's not possible to go farther without driving into the sea, I should think the answer is obvious. Now may we be permitted to continue on our way, before the young lady

11

receives a chill from this confounded gale which is raging through the coach?'

The Lieutenant saluted.

'As you wish, sir, but my advice to you is not to pick up any strangers you might see walking the road.'

'Is it indeed? On a night like this it would be inhuman to leave a leper to fend for himself. I think it highly unlikely that we shall meet anyone, but if we do, I assure you we shall offer them shelter from the elements. However, should your fears be confirmed and that person prove to be an escaped prisoner, then you have my word that he shall be handed over to your garrison the moment we reach Marshsea. Meantime, I bid you adieu, Lieutenant.'

Mr. Layton closed the window and resumed his seat as the horses were whipped into motion.

'I trust you have not become too frozen by that encounter?' he said, brushing the snow from his coat.

'The open window did little to improve my comfort, but I suppose the Lieutenant was only doing his duty.'

'A deuce too seriously in my opinion. There's little enough chance of prisoners travelling this way. South is a deal more likely. It's nearer to France and, as everyone knows, the Kentish coast is a haven for smugglers.'

'Many think East Anglia more likely. They say the rough fenmen are uppermost in assisting the escapes.'

'Indeed,' he said, glancing shrewdly at me. 'How came you by such intelligence?'

'My step-mother was talking of it before I left. She told me of the lawlessness of this corner of England,' I replied, deeming it wisest not to mention that she also considered Grandpa not above such treasonable activities, providing there was sufficient money to be gained from the enterprise. Though how she could know such a thing, without having met him, was beyond me.

'You live in the fens then?'

'No. My step-mother has a farm just outside London. At Kensington.'

'If you'll forgive the comment, this is surely a most unfashionable time to go visiting.'

'It's no social jaunt which brings me this way, I assure you. Marshsea is to be my future home.'

To show I wished to end the conversation I turned my attention to the window. It was quite dark now and I could see little in the faint light cast by the horn lantern fastened to the coach's side. Now the immediate danger of being robbed was over, I was concerned for my ring's safety. It would be embarrassing to remove my calash while watched by a complete stranger, yet I would know no serenity until the ring was once more on my finger. I wished he would return to his own preoccupation so I could retrieve it discreetly. As though reading my thoughts he smiled and said:

'If it'll make you any happier, I'll look the other way whilst you retrieve your ring. Though why a lady should be so self-conscious about removing her calash I cannot conceive.'

To my annoyance I blushed as I met his eyes. 'I didn't realize you saw me hide it.'

'I happened to look round as you were pushing it into your hair. I thought it an admirable hiding place.'

Relieved that I need no longer pretend, I uncovered my head, but my embarrassment was not over. The more I tried to remove the ring the more firmly it became entangled in my hair.

'May I be of assistance?'

With surprising gentleness he extracted the ring and held it admiringly between his stubby fingers.

'It is indeed beautiful and valuable too, if I'm any judge.'

His eyes glanced critically at my travelling coat. Although I had spent many hours steaming it, the worn cuffs and the crushed pile clearly indicated its age.

"It's my engagement ring,' I said, feeling an explanation was necessary.

'Indeed? Your fiancé must be an exceedingly wealthy man.'

'My grandfather says he is.'

'Surely you know?'

'I haven't yet had the pleasure of making Mr. Cheval's acquaintance, though I'm assured he's a most agreeable gentleman. The marriage was arranged by my grand-father.'

'Not Mr. Rolf Cheval of Marsh House?'

'Indeed yes.'

'You are to marry him!'

His incredulity was evident and I was annoyed that he so obviously considered me not grand enough for the honour.

'Is he a friend of yours?'

'No.' He spoke sharply. 'I know his name, but we have not met.'

'How disappointing. For a moment I thought you might be able to tell me something of him. Grandpa's letters were inclined to be brief.'

'I know little except he's reputed to be the biggest ship owner in East Anglia. His brigs carry the coal down from Newcastle, but I expect you already know that.'

'I know you are mistaken,' I replied, still annoyed by his appraisal of my clothes. 'Grandpa is the biggest ship owner.'

The retort hit well. I was delighted by the look of amazement which covered his countenance.

'Not Silas Hawkins? That's impossible. I've always understood that a feud existed betwixt the two families. A bitter one by all accounts.'

'That's true. Papa often talked of it. He told me how the two families were partners until they quarrelled over the running of the fleet. Then Jeremiah Cheval, my fiancé's great-grandfather, took four of the ships and formed his own company. He became a most bitter rival. Now both Grandpa and my fiancé have decided that the feud is nothing but a handicap and wish to be free of it. They decided that the most satisfactory way was to unite the two families.'

'So you're to be sacrificed.'

'That's not the word I would choose. Most of the better marriages are arranged for family reasons, you know.'

'Without the two people most concerned ever having met? How can you be sure you're suited?'

'The Prince of Wales didn't see Princess Caroline until after the marriage was arranged.'

'And we all know the result of that alliance. Surely that should serve as a warning to all serious-minded people. In my opinion, you'd do well to learn a great deal more about your fiancé before committing yourself.'

His presumptuous manner was irritating.

'Are you suggesting there's a reason why I might repent the marriage?'

'I'm merely giving you the advice I'd offer any young lady in similar circumstances.'

'Indeed. Then you have my assurance that I'm well able to take care of myself.'

'Now I have annoyed you. That was not my intention.'

'On the contrary, I appreciate your advice, though in this instance it's unnecessary. Most young ladies would consider themselves fortunate in having such an excellent match arranged for them, and I'm no exception. If my marriage is also instrumental in breaching the gulf between the two families and thereby preventing further bloodshed, then I'm doubly pleased. They say that respect for one's husband breeds love.'

Though I forced myself to sound confident, I would have preferred to quiz Mr. Layton more about my unknown fiancé. However, as he obviously had such a poor opinion of all arranged marriages, I deemed it wiser to end the conversation.

2

The night was dark as the horn announced our arrival at Marshsea. As the coach slid to a halt in the cobbled yard of the Dog and Partridge, an ostler came towards us with a pole lantern. The horses neighed and set their brasses jangling. Mr. Layton stood up and, with the ostler's aid, successfully negotiated the ice covered steps.

'Take care, they're dangerous,' he said, turning to assist me.

As I stepped onto the frozen iron I realized how right he was. My foot slid from under me and, but for his support, I would have fallen.

'Hold my arm,' he said. 'I'll assist you to the tavern. The ostler will see to our boxes.'

'Mr. Hawkins was expecting me to arrive yesterday. I do hope there's still someone here to meet me,' I said, peering into the darkness hoping to see a coach, but there was not even a gig in sight. 'Perhaps the carriage is waiting in an outhouse,' I added hopefully.

'I doubt that,' Mr. Layton said, opening the door for me. 'This is a town hostelry and will have barely sufficient stabling for the horses.'

We entered a passage lit by a single sconce. Beside a narrow staircase stood a small table containing candlesticks and a large brass bell. Mr. Layton rang the bell and we brushed the snow from our clothes as we waited. He rang again.

'Where the devil is the man?' he asked. 'He must know of our arrival by now.'

There were sounds of voices coming from beyond a door at the end of the passage. Mr. Layton strode towards it and pushed it open. Not wishing to be left alone, I followed him. The room was smokefilled and reeked with the stench of stale tobacco. The ceiling was so low it almost touched Mr. Layton's head. The walls were filthy and the oak beams festooned with dusty spiders' webs. The straw covering the floor was reduced to a soggy mush by the soaked boots which had trampled it.

On benches round the ingle-nook sat a dozen surly looking men, who stopped talking as we entered. For an instant I had the impression that the biggest of them was about to call a greeting, then his expression changed and he stared at us as unsmiling as the others. Seeing them reminded me of old Daniel's stories of barbarous pirates, and I was indeed glad of Mr. Layton's protective presence.

Two of the men wore smocks over their corded

16

trousers, which had once been brown but were now bleached the colour of rotting hay. The others wore shapeless woollen garments, which fastened at the neck and hung over their trousers more like sacks than shirts. To complete their ensembles they wore thigh length boots and pointed woollen caps.

With the exception of the youngest, who looked little more than twelve years old, and the eldest, whose weather-worn face gave him the appearance of having already seen his century, all had black beards. Though whether the colour was natural, or merely the accumulation of many years' grime, it was difficult to guess. They looked too poor to be able to afford the grog they held in their coarse hands; yet each wore gold earrings which glittered in the firelight.

'Good evening, gentlemen.'

They returned Mr. Layton's greeting with sullen stares.

'Is the host to be found? The night is raw, with a deal more snow to come, I fancy.'

His pleasantry brought no change to their unfriendly faces.

'Is there another bell?' I asked, glancing at the wooden counter on which stood a large barrel and several pewter tankards.

As I spoke one of the watchers heaved himself to his feet. He was heavy as an ape and, being too tall to stand upright in the low room, he crossed towards the trap-door behind the counter with a bent, loping gait.

'Jake.' His great voice bellowed down into the cellar. 'There be travellers here.'

Mr. Layton guided me nearer the fire, but no-one moved to allow us to share its warmth.

Mr. Layton appeared unperturbed by our hostile reception, yet I dreaded to contemplate how I might have fared had I faced these men alone. I was annoyed that Grandpa had not protected me from such a possibility.

Presently Jake, a small, rotund man, came up the cellar ladder. He beamed angelically at us and was such a vivid contrast to his customers, that I wanted to laugh from sheer relief.

17

'A room has been reserved for me, I believe,' Mr. Layton said, cutting short the landlord's profuse greeting. 'My name is Layton.'

Jake frowned. 'That is so. The fire was lit nigh on two hours ago, so the room should be warm enough by now, but nothing was said about a young lady.'

'This is Miss Debnam. Her grandfather, Mr. Silas Hawkins, is to meet her here. Pray have the goodness to inform him of her arrival.'

Jake scratched his thinning hair. 'There be some mistake. Nobody be waiting here for her.'

'But there must be,' I said. 'I know I was expected last night, but surely Mr. Hawkins realized that I was merely delayed and would come at the earliest opportunity.'

'Nobody was waiting here for you last night neither.'

'Are you sure?' Mr. Layton asked.

'Nobody from the Hall has been here for over a week now. Not Mr. Hawkins nor none of his men.'

The news was perplexing. I had been so certain someone would be waiting to greet me.

'Then how am I to reach the Hall? Have you a carriage for hire?' I asked, wondering what manner of man Grandpa was to place me in this embarrassing position.

'No, ma'am. Only a fool would attempt that sea road in a blizzard.'

'Then what am I to do?'

'Stay here, that be all 'e can do. Lucky I have a spare room. It be not much used this time o' year, but a fire soon takes the chill off.'

The thought of spending the night in the vicinity of these villainous looking men brought a chill to my spine. Yet I had no choice.

'You are most kind,' I said, speaking with more composure than I felt. 'I shall be grateful for a night's lodgings.'

'Have Miss Debnam's boxes taken to my room,' Mr. Layton ordered. 'It'll be warmer for her there. The other room will do admirably for me.'

'I can't possibly allow that,' I protested. 'It's I who has caused the upset, therefore I must make do with the unused room.'

18

'Nonsense. I insist. A cold room is of little consequence to me, so no further argument, if you please.'

Jake lit another candle from the one on the counter and opened the door at the far end of the bar. Before us was another narrow passage. At the end a flight of steps, so steep as to be almost perpendicular, disappeared into the darkness above. They culminated in a tiny landing. There were only two doors and Jake opened the one at the far end.

The room was pleasant, with firelight flickering over the floral curtains and canopied bed. Yet, there was a dank chill in the atmosphere. Jake lit the candle standing on the washing stand.

'Your room is next door, sir,' he said, turning to Mr. Layton. 'This way, if you please. The pot-boy will bring your boxes up in a minute, ma'am.'

I watched the door close behind them with a sense of apprehension. It was strange to think I had once been concerned at the thought of travelling alone in a closed carriage with Mr. Layton and was now regarding him as a trusted friend. Normally I am not easily given to making casual friendships, yet something about Mr. Layton's personality forced me to like him.

As I washed my face with the cold water tipped from the earthenware jug, I remembered his advice about my forthcoming marriage. If Grandpa was so lax about my arrival here, might he not be even more callous in his choice of a husband for me? I tried to laugh at the fear, but it was still niggling my thoughts when someone knocked upon the door. Thinking it to be a pot-boy with my box, I called an invitation to enter.

Mr. Layton stood in the doorway.

'We appear to be the only travellers here tonight, so I wondered if you would honour me with your company for dinner?'

I noticed how much slimmer he looked now he was without his Garrick top coat.

'Oh, I think not . . . I had planned to dine in my chamber.'

I wished I could accept his invitation, for this room

was doing little to warm my chilled bones. Yet only loose women accepted such invitations unchaperoned.

As though reading my thoughts, he said 'I realize we shall be bending the rules of etiquette somewhat, but in the circumstances I think it permissible. It would be foolish for each of us to dine alone when we might have the pleasure of agreeable company. Please say you will?'

He looked so pleading as the candle-light flickered over his curly, brown hair, and so little like the dour stranger who had boarded the coach at Wisbech, that I could not refuse.

Upon arriving downstairs, I noticed that the small table, placed by the fire in the private parlour, was prepared for two.

The meal was excellent. Though we had stopped for a mid-day meal at Lynn, I had eaten little, and so was able to do full justice to the delicious duckling soaked in orange sauce.

'Shall we finish with apple dumplings, followed by a glass of good brandy?' he asked, as our empty plates were removed by Jake's buxom wife. 'It will help you to sleep.'

'Brandy? I thought there was none left in the country. The war has lasted so long.'

'There is plenty in these parts, I wager. Silks and tea too, likely as not.'

'Smuggled you mean?'

He smiled. 'Never ask questions in the fens. Not if you want to stay out of trouble. The fen tigers are funny folk. They have laws of their own. Many an inquisitor has vanished from these parts.'

'Surely not murdered?'

He shrugged. 'Swamps and quicksands hide their secrets. People disappear. Maybe they go away of their own accord when their questions are not answered; maybe not. Each man minds his own business and asks no questions of his neighbours.'

'That is not a very friendly way to live.'

'It is their way.'

'Are you a "tiger", did you call them?'

20

'No. I am not of the fens.'

'Yet, you know about them. Have you been here many times?'

'Asking questions is a habit I must not encourage. Tell me more of this old Daniel who meant so much to you.'

As we talked I became aware of a sense of contentment. The conversation flowed easily, and it became difficult to realize that we had met for the first time that day. I felt as though I had known him many years. Suddenly I wished that tomorrow and our parting would never come.

'Why such a solemn look?' he asked.

I blushed. 'I was thinking how easily we talk together. We might be old friends instead of mere acquaintances.'

'You feel the companionship too? That pleases me.' To my surprise he leaned across the table and laid his hand over mine. 'I trust you'll always regard me as a friend, even though we were not formally introduced. Please remember that if you should ever need assistance, you can rely on me. I expect to be staying in the district for several weeks, so if the need should arise, just leave a message with Jake. He'll see it reaches me.'

His offer was made all the more puzzling by the intensity of his voice. Once again I had the impression that he knew something more than he would admit about my future life.

'Have you some reason for thinking I might need help?'

His face remained inscrutable.

'No-one can foresee the future or when they are likely to need a friend. Tonight is an excellent example. Who could foresee the blizzard and your grandfather's inability to meet you?'

'Has Jake said something to you about Grandpa?'

'Gad no. Whatever gave you that idea?'

'I just wondered,' I replied, realizing I liked this stranger very much, perhaps better than anyone I knew.

Yet, as always, his answers were evasive. I knew little more about him now, than when he had boarded the stagecoach. For the first time that evening the conversation faltered. To restart it I asked how long he thought the blizzard would last.

Though I was reluctant to end our tête-à-tête, and stayed talking for almost another hour, the sparkle had vanished. I returned to my chamber feeling vaguely disappointed.

During my absence someone had replenished the fire and the room was much warmer. The wooden chest containing all my possessions now stood beside the whitewashed wall.

Feeling too stimulated to sleep, I sat by the fire recalling the evening's memories. Earlier I had been annoyed at Grandpa's failure to meet me, but now I was glad, for it had made possible an interlude I would long remember.

When I became pleasantly drowsy I took the key from my reticule and inserted it in the lock of my box. Though it had turned easily this morning, it now refused to move. The box had been exposed to the blizzard and I realized the dampness was causing the lock to stick. Nothing annoyed me more than to be forced into admitting that my strength was unequal to a task, yet it became increasingly obvious that I must seek a gentleman's assistance if I wished to acquire my night clothes.

Thinking it strange that I should need Mr. Layton's help so soon after his offer, I took the candle from the mantelshelf and stepped from my chamber. The landing outside was black as a widow's dress and the candlelight threw my elongated shadow onto the wall, making it so tall the head curved over the ceiling.

I knocked on Mr. Layton's door and waited, but there was no movement from within. Thinking he might be asleep I knocked harder. Then I knocked twice more. Still there was no answer.

Perhaps I should have gone away but it seemed so strange that anyone could sleep through such heavy knocking, that I turned the knob. The door opened.

'Are you there, Mr. Layton?'

An unexpected draught caught the door and pulled it from my hand, and also blew out my candleflame, but by the fire-light, I could see the room was unoccupied. Thinking he had merely gone downstairs for a forgotten article I decided to wait for him to return. When half an hour passed and he still did not come, I decided to go downstairs in search of the landlord's help.

The tavern was hushed as I negotiated the steep staircase. The candle which had earlier cast a glimmer of light along the bottom corridor was now extinguished, and the draught was causing mine to flicker so badly I was afraid it would be blown out. I found the room where we had dined earlier, but that too was in darkness. The silence in the tavern was absolute, giving the uncanny feeling that the walls were watching, spying on the stranger who dared to disturb their peace. The room where the sailors had earlier drunk their grog was also empty, though here the fire still burned brightly enough to cast a cosy glow over the vacant wooden benches.

It was obvious that during the short time I had sat by the fire in my chamber Jake had made the tavern safe for the night and gone to his own quarters.

Yet where was Mr. Layton?

Puzzled by my inability to find him I returned upstairs. His chamber door was still standing open and I could not resist the temptation to step inside. Apart from his box standing by the wall, the room had every appearance of being unoccupied. None of his personal possessions were as yet unpacked. By now curiosity had completely supplanted my manners. I crossed to the clothes closet and opened the door. That too was empty. Not even his hat or Garrick coat hung on the pegs.

3

The blizzard had ceased when the maid brought me some washing water the following morning. After she left I threw back the sheets and sheepskin rug and crossed to the window for my first daylight glimpse of Marshsea.

My room overlooked a crooked cobbled side street. Already several housewives were busily knocking snow from their window ledges. By the cross roads a group of children were throwing snowballs at the shop signs and shieking with laughter as they scored hits and spattered snow over the flintstone walls.

In the next room Mr. Layton was singing lustily and I wondered when he had returned. Certainly well after midnight for, although I had no means of telling the exact time, I had lain awake on the oat-chaff mattress for at least an hour after my search for him.

I washed quickly in the tepid water, for the fire was out and the room quite chilly. I was glad to pull my woollen dress over the underclothes I had been forced to sleep in.

Deciding to have another try to open the box, I took the key from the toilet table and inserted it in the lock. It had dried during the night and now the catch turned easily. I was glad I had tried it before again seeking Mr. Layton's assistance.

The temperature of the room did not encourage finicky beautifying. In record time I brushed my hair, fastened it into a chignon, added a little lavender water behind my ears, and relocked my box.

Mr. Layton was already in the private parlour when I arrived downstairs. He terminated his conversation with Jake abruptly.

'I trust you slept well,' he said, placing a chair near the fire for me.

'Thank you, yes . . . and you?'

'Excellently.'

I was longing to mention my search for him and ask where he went on such a foul night. Instead I said:

'I thought I heard you go downstairs soon after we retired.'

His smile was unfaltering. 'There are many creaks in old buildings, especially those made of lath and plaster. The oak beams contract as the room cools. It's best to ignore them. Come to the fire whilst Jake prepares our breakfast. What would you like? Ham; mutton; cheese; eggs?'

Feeling disappointed that he should lie to me, even indirectly, I chose ham followed by hot chocolate. I asked if Grandpa or a groom had arrived yet.

'No, ma'am,' Jake replied. 'No-one has called this morning. I reckon the snow be putting folk off. It lies nigh on two feet deep.'

'Don't look so downhearted,' Mr. Layton said, as Jake left us. 'The tavern is a pleasant enough place to wait.'

'I cannot understand why Grandpa hasn't sent a message. After all, I'm travelling on his instruction. Do you think it possible that he's ill?'

'Possibly but unlikely. I'm told he's never suffered a day's illness. The fen folk are tough. They have to be. Only the strongest can survive in this water-logged climate.' Mr. Layton stretched his booted legs nearer the fire. 'Can you ride a horse?'

'I lived on a farm, and rode before I could roll a hoop.'

'Then if no-one's come for you by the time our breakfast is over, I'll hire a couple of sturdy nags and escort you to the Hall. I'd suggest a carriage, but I doubt if it would survive long on these roads today.'

'You are indeed kind, but I cannot trespass further on your generosity. If you will but point the way I shall manage quite admirably.'

'This is no morning for riding alone. A wrong step could plunge you into a dyke faster than a heron's swoop.'

'But have you not commitments of your own?' I demurred, though I was secretly pleased at the prospect of another journey with him, thus delaying our final parting.

'Nothing so urgent it will spoil for waiting.'

By ten thirty he had hired the horses and they were trudging through the snow at their own easy pace. As we turned North along the cliff road, I had my first glimpse of the sea. A great sheet of tarnished silver stretching as far as the eye could see. Below us a strip of beach was washed clear of snow by the receding tide. Fishing boats were bobbing towards the harbour. Nearer the horizon the brigs glided like buxom ladies, their red

25

sails billowing majestically. It was frightening to remember that, across this peaceful scene, was war-ravaged Europe and, had Britain not been an island, it too might have been crushed beneath the ravenous greed of Napoleon. I shuddered and turned my attention inland.

The countryside lay before me like a great white table top and I knew now why no-one would risk this road in a blizzard and why Papa had called it, 'the devil's own corner'. When a gale swept across this great plain, there was nothing to break its anger. It would come roaring along with hellish fury, destroying all that stood against it.

'It's a desolate scene,' I said.

'Aye, though it appears quiet enough at the moment, but when the fens slumber take care, there's always danger lurking. The sands over there for instance. The stretch between the two crosses.' He pointed northwards with his riding crop. 'Never go wandering there alone, for they mark the quicksands and out there near the horizon are the sandbanks. Many of our finest ships, aye, and men too, draw their last breath there on a windy night.' He paused, then added, 'But away with unpleasantness. I declare the sun has an almost spring-like warmth.'

For a while we enjoyed the refreshing morning in companionable silence, then I asked:

'What do you know of Grandpa? Is he really the ogre my step-mother suggests?'

'I've never met him, but from all accounts he's an upright man. A hard worker and honest—at least by his own standards—and he expects those about him to be likewise.'

'Are you suggesting his standards are not always honest?'

'This is a remote part of England. The men here set their own code, one which may seem strange to a town dandy. Yet, in their own way, the tigers are honest. One could go away for a month and leave the house unlocked. Nothing would be stolen. Quite the contrary. On his return the traveller would most likely find a dish of eggs

26

or a poached rabbit waiting on the parlour table to welcome him back. Leastways so my sister said.'

'Does she live in these parts?'

'She did before her death.'

'I'm sorry,' I said, hoping he might tell me more of her. Instead the morose look closed over his face and we rode in silence.

The slight breeze stung colour into my cheeks. Soon now my new life would begin. I would become part of this strange community of fenmen. With every step my engagement to Mr. Cheval was becoming more a reality. Soon I would be able to judge him for myself.

'Tell me of my financé? Is he young or old?'

'Don't you even know that?' His brown eyes regarded me quizzically. 'For a prospective bride your knowledge of him is abysmally inadequate. He's not in the first bloom of manhood, but neither is he old,' he added, as my smile faded.

'Is he well liked?'

'It's not always possible for a rich man to be popular . . . Have you noticed the numerous windmills and dykes? The waterways were cut by the Dutchmen who drained the fens. In olden days all this was underwater. When it drained away in summer the grasses grew so tall, the men had to walk on stilts to see over it. Even now the tigers are sometimes called the "ten foot men".'

Mr. Layton's abrupt change of subject puzzled me and I wondered why he avoided questions about Mr. Cheval.

'This is where I must leave you,' he said, as the Hall gates, and cottage where the keeper lived, came into view.

'Oh, but you must allow me to introduce you to Grandpa. I'm sure he'll wish to offer you refreshment.'

'My regrets, but that is impossible. I must be on my way. The lodge keeper will doubtless see you safely to the house.'

'But the mare?'

'She can be returned to the tavern when your boxes are collected. Not many folk will wish to ride today.'

We halted by the gates.

'Then I can but give you my most sincere thanks for your assistance. I am indeed greatly indebted to you.'

He grasped my hand warmly.

'The pleasure's entirely mine. Don't forget, if you ever need help you must come straight to me. Promise?'

Again his voice was disconcertingly intense.

'I promise, though I trust I shall soon be in the position to repay your generosity, and not impose further on it.'

I watched him ride away feeling as if I were losing a good friend. I sighed, regretting that I would probably never see him again. Then I turned resolutely to the rusty chain hanging by the gate and tugged until the corroded bell clanged. The gateman appeared, wiping his hands on a coarse towel. He was about fifty and his sandy coloured beard gave his face a sunny glow. Like the sailors, he too was wearing earrings, though his were of a duller metal. He stood unsmiling in the cottage doorway.

'Good morning,' I said. 'Pray open the gates. I'm Miss Debnam.'

'You can't come in here. The Squire said I was not to admit nobody.'

Last night I was annoyed at finding no-one waiting for me at the tavern. Now this man's effrontery was not to be endured.

'Kindly open these gates immediately or it will be the worse for you. Mr. Hawkins is my grandfather and I'm positive that, whatever your orders, they do not include me.'

For a moment longer he stood staring, then he turned back into the cottage. Thinking he had decided to end the matter, I was about to tug at the bell chain again when he reappeared with a large iron key in his hand.

'Hope I be doing right,' he muttered. 'The Squire said no-one was to pass.'

'Then I will accept the responsibility.'

I set the mare at a steady jog along the carriageway. Presently we rounded the bend and there before me was the Hall. A squat three storey building of grey bricks, built more for convenience than beauty. Only three steps led up to the studded oak storm door. This was flanked on either side by leaded windows.

I dismounted and fastened the reins to a hitching post. The resounding clangs of the door bell echoed as through a vault. Presently wooden clogs clattered over a stone floor. The door opened a few inches and a young maid peered through the resulting cleft.

'I'm Miss Henrietta Debnam. Pray allow me to enter.'

'I daresn't do that.'

This latest piece of insolence was too much. I had travelled over a hundred miles in foul weather to comply with Grandpa's request, and now I was being treated as an interloper.

'You dare not! How mean you? Have I not said that I'm Miss Debnam. Open the door this instant and inform Mr. Hawkins of my arrival.'

'I daresn't let you in, not even if you were Queen Charlotte herself.'

'What nonsense. Allow me in immediately or I shall insist upon your dismissal.'

I tried to push the door open wider, but it was held in place by an iron chain.

'I best fetch Mrs. Gawthrop,' she said.

Mr. Layton had warned me that fen folk had peculiar ways but surely even they were not accustomed to treating visitors with such lack of courtesy. I stamped my feet to warm them and my anger mounted with each passing minute.

That I should travel all this way to marry Mr. Cheval was my grandfather's idea, not mine. Though I had agreed willingly enough, I was not a docile miss who would submit to insults, as he would quickly learn.

At last I heard returning footsteps. The door closed for a moment, then opened wide enough for me to enter.

'Is this your normal way of treating visitors?' I asked, stepping into the square vestibule where a log fire, burning in the large fireplace, helped to dispel some of the gloom.

'I am right sorry about that,' said the woman, dressed

entirely in black, even to her mob cap, who I guessed to be Mrs. Gawthrop. 'You must forgive Sarah. She is new here. Even so, she should have realized an exception must be made in your case, but the truth is, no-one was expecting you.'

'How can that be? My grandfather explicitly asked me to arrive on the 27th, and but for a mishap I would have been here. It was annoying enough to find no-one waiting for me at the tavern. To be told I'm not expected is outrageous.'

'Didn't you receive the master's second letter? The one telling you not to come. He sent it soon as he knew.'

'I received none since the one telling me when to arrive.'

She shook her grey head. 'My poor child, it's not surprising you're vexed. The weather's been that bad these last few days it must have delayed the mails. You don't know of our affliction then?'

Her voice alarmed me. 'What's happened? Is it Grandpa?'

'Bless you no. He's hale enough for two men. Young Mary, the kitchen maid, is the one. She went to tend her sick mother. The silly young goose never told us it was smallpox. Back here she came bold as a robin and brought the dratted disease with her. Here! Into the Hall itself!'

'Oh, no.'

My cry of pity was instantaneous. Old Daniel had once had smallpox and now the deep pits on his face were a revolting sight. Yet he counted himself fortunate to have survived the epidemic.

'Now you understand why the master gave orders that no-one was to be admitted. He wants to stop the disease spreading to Marshsea. He made us all submit to this new cowpox vaccine.'

'Then you have little to worry about. Its protection is perfect.'

'Can we be sure? Some say it protects. Others say, if it is anything like the old inoculation, it will make us more likely to catch smallpox, but come you to the fire.

You must be frozen waiting on the step such a hoary morning. I'll tell the master of your arrival, but don't go near a soul. I'm not sure I did the right thing in admitting you.'

I was indeed glad to move nearer the blaze, which sent sparks up a wide chimney. The vestibule was about twelve feet square, with great black oak furniture soaking up the light and panelled walls decorated with an assortment of tarnished pikes and swords. This was a man's abode, completely lacking feminine charm. I wondered what Grandpa was like. To judge from the house, not a man much given to personal comfort.

Mrs. Gawthrop had barely entered the room on my left, before the door crashed open again and I was facing a big man whose beard was as white as his hair. For a moment he looked at me, his piercing blue eyes missing no detail of my appearance. Then he was across the room and hugging me in such a bear-like grip the breath was squeezed from me.

'Henrietta, lass, it's good to see 'e. You should have sent a messenger from the tavern. These roads are not fit for a gal alone on horseback.'

His grip relaxed and I was pushed to arm's length for another scrutiny.

'You have your mother's black hair and brown eyes, otherwise there is little similarity. She was dainty as a kitten.'

There was a trace of sadness in his gruff voice. Thinking to add comfort, I said:

'You are also tall. Mayhap I inherited a little from you.'

'Aye, mayhap. Either way it's good to see 'e, lass. These old quarrels are better buried. They do good to no-one and bring nought but misery. Yet, your arrival is ill-timed, I fear. I would not die happy if this clear skin was ruined by smallpox. Mrs. Gawthrop tells me my second letter arrived not.'

'It matters little. I was vaccinated during the outbreak at home two years ago, so I shall be quite safe.'

'Nay, lass. That's something we can't know for sure. I tell the servants that Doctor Jenner's vaccine will keep

31

them safe, but in my heart I'm fearful. We who are here must stay, but you must not share the danger, vaccine or no.'

'There's no danger. None of those vaccinated at home caught it.'

'Nevertheless, I cannot rest easy with you in the Hall. When the trouble is over you shall treat this as your home until you become Mistress of Marsh House. Meanwhile, I must make other arrangements for you. There are two alternatives. Either you can return to the Dog and Partridge, where you shall have every comfort your heart can desire . . .'

'Oh, no. Not that,' I cried, remembering my dismal chamber and the aggressive looking sailors.

'Then you must go to Marsh House. Mr. Cheval will be as eager as I to prevent you catching smallpox.'

'That's impossible. Mr. Cheval and I are strangers. Not yet introduced. He may not even like me when we meet . . . or I him, for that matter,' I added, determined Grandpa should realize that I too intended having a say in the matter if Mr. Cheval was repugnant.

'How could he not like the owner of such a pretty face? You are more comely than even I dared to hope, though I described you in glowing enough terms,' he chuckled. 'You just make yourself comfortable whilst I change into my riding clothes. I'll get Mrs. Gawthrop to bring you a warming drink whilst you wait.'

'I would rather stay here with you.'

'That's not possible in the circumstances, but have no fear, Mr. Cheval will be only too pleased to provide you with temporary accommodation.'

4

The sun was shining directly onto our faces as we rode back towards Marshsea and the snow was trampled to a slushy mess. On the shimmering sea the brigs still glided confidently towards the harbour.

'Are any of them yours?' I asked.

'Those flying the blue flag. Capital ships, every last one of them.'

Of those nearest to the shore I could see two flying his emblem. My heart filled with pride as I realized that they would one day belong to the son I hoped to conceive.

'What of the fishing vessels? Are they yours too?'

'They mostly belong to Marshsea folk. They're late coming in today. Reckon as how they were blown off course last night and sheltered down the coast. At Whitesea most like. The sandbanks there make a natural haven for the smaller boats, though my captains curse them. Many a good brig has died there. They say enough lost coal is scattered over those sands to start a mine.'

'Have you lost any?'

'We all have, and good men too. The worst part in the old days was knowing your men were out there drowning and nothing could be done to save them. Sometimes they clung to the rigging of a sinking ship for nigh on two days, knowing all the time there was not a hope in hell of being saved unless the wind dropped. It broke a body's heart to see them. Things are different now we have a lifesaving boat. They stand a fighting chance these days.'

The town, which was almost deserted when I passed through it with Mr. Layton, was now hustling with activity. By the cobbled harbour wall anxious fishwives shielded their eyes and scanned the sea for their husbands' boats. In mid-stream, the barges were fussing round a brig which stood with its masts stark against the blue sky.

Tradesmen were clearing snow from their shop fronts and on the white greensward near the barracks, soldiers in scarlet and black were practising musket drill.

'Waste of time,' Grandpa commented. 'Might as well go back to their farms and families. Boney's had his tail clipped too short by the Tsar's men to worry about invading us now. Look you there,' he added, pointing to a brig now entering the harbour. 'That's one of the Cheval fleet. You can tell it by the red star on the blue flag. The star was added when the feud started. Ah, lass, I shall die happy when they all sail under the same flag again.'

'Who suggested uniting the two families?'

Grandpa chuckled. It was a deep throated sound which rumbled inside his chest.

'Your fiancé will doubtless claim that honour.'

'But you thought it a good idea?'

Again he chuckled and I had the impression that he had played a larger part in bringing about the arrangement than he was prepared to admit.

'Aye. I agreed right enough. The bargain was good.'

'Does it not worry you that the name of Hawkins will be swallowed by that of Cheval?' I asked, as we left the town.

'What's a name? You know what that Shakespeare fellow said.'

This puzzled me. Grandpa was riding along smiling as happily as if he was inheriting a fortune, instead of handing one to his rival. Yet he was supposed to be an astute business man.

'I fail to understand why you consider it a good bargain. Mr. Cheval has everything to gain—you nothing. I can see well enough why he suggested it.'

'True, providing I die first, but that need not necessarily be so. The agreement says that whichever of us lives the longest shall manage both fleets until your son comes of age. Of course, should Mr. Cheval die before the child is born you, as his widow, will inherit the fleet.'

34

'Supposing I die first without having a son?'

'Then naturally the agreement becomes void.'

'It still seems unfair. You're twice his age . . . at least, I was told he's comparatively young. Is that not true?'

Grandpa smiled at my concern. 'Have no fear. You're not to be an old man's darling. Mr. Cheval is handsome enough to quicken the heart of any romantic wench. Many a local gal would gladly fit your shoes and many a dowager will not sleep happily when this news is let fly.'

We crossed a narrow pack bridge in single file and soon came to an open gate with Marsh House worked into the tracery. In the distance I could see a magnificent Renaissance style house, with three floors of large symmetrical windows and miniature replicas for the attics above. A flight of steps, with a graceful balustrade, led to the huge oak door, while the ivy around the four portico columns added a pleasing touch of green.

Grandpa saw me gazing up at the glass dome protruding from the pantile roof.

'A hundred candles burn up there each night the Cheval ships are due in harbour,' he said. 'All the windows face seaward. The other side is lined with metal and burnished everyday to reflect the maximum light.' He chuckled. 'My captains also use it and it doesn't cost me a groat.'

'What's he like?'

'You'll see soon enough now, lass.'

I glanced down at my coat. The pile was crushed from travelling. The skirt bespattered with mud and dirty where the other passengers' wet baskets had rubbed against it. My appearance was not likely to encourage praise from the one person I most wanted to impress.

This was a far different meeting from the one I had visualized, for that had taken place at the Hall. A carefully planned dinner party, where I would greet him filled with the confidence of knowing I looked well groomed.

For a moment I was annoyed with Grandpa for insisting upon this undignified introduction. Then I acknowledged he was doing his best in a difficult situation, and hoped that Mr. Cheval would not be too disappointed with me. It would be so humiliating to be sent back to the farm still a spinster.

My hands were trembling as we stopped by the steps and a lackey hurried to help me to dismount.

'Is your master at home?' Grandpa asked.

'I believe so, sir.'

'That means you know damned well he is. Come on, m'girl, this way.'

Grandpa's hand was beneath my arm propelling me towards the open door, where the butler was waiting to greet us.

'Good afternoon, sir, madam,' he said bowing.

He showed no surprise at our unexpected arrival. In fact, to judge from his manner, we might have been invited guests.

'Mr. Cheval is in the library, sir. He's been informed of your arrival.'

'I'll wager he has,' Grandpa retorted. 'This establishment has a better look-out than the barracks.'

'We do our best to welcome visitors, sir.'

As I followed him across the small ante-room I was possessed by a desire to run away. Yet, at the same time, I was anxious to meet Mr. Cheval, to see for myself that he was not old, obese, or made hideous by smallpox. When the butler opened the library door my hands were wet with fright. I took a deep breath and entered the room.

Mr. Cheval was standing by the fire, one hand resting on the white marble mantelshelf. Across the width of the sumptuous room his eyes engaged mine, then he came towards me with a grace born of luxurious living and was, without doubt, the most handsome man I had met. Tall and slender with black hair waving back from a widow's peak and curling neatly below his ears. His eyes were neither blue nor green, but a mixture of each, and appeared to change colour with each particle of reflected light. Grandpa moved closer.

'Permit me to introduce my grand-daughter. Miss Henrietta Debnam. Henrietta, may I present Mr. Rolf Cheval.'

'Your most humble servant, ma'am.'

'Yours, sir,' I said, noticing his elegant bow.

'This is indeed a pleasure,' he replied, extending his hand to assist me rise from the curtsy. 'An unforeseen honour to warm this frozen day.'

His voice was pleasing and contained none of the long vowels I was beginning to associate with the fens.

'Is she not comely?' Grandpa sounded pleased with himself. 'Come, m'boy, are you not pleased with our bargain?'

The colour flushed into my face; I could feel it flooding scarlet down my neck. Grandpa's remarks were meant kindly, but they made me feel like a prized animal that was being sold.

'Indeed, I am the most fortunate of men. Your beauty, m'dear, surpasses my most lavish expectations.'

I looked at him, expecting to see a teasing twinkle in those striking eyes, but they were quite serious.

'It is I who am honoured, sir.'

'Sir?' His eyebrow lifted quizzically. 'Are we not to become better acquainted than that. My name is Rolf, you know.'

Grandpa watched approvingly as he led me to a blue and gold davenport and positioned a beautifully embroidered pole screen to protect my face from the fire's heat.

'I take it that you are well satisfied?' Grandpa said, flicking up his coat tails and seating himself.

'Indeed yes, she is perfect.'

I wished they would stop referring to me as something being bought and sold. Though I knew the marriage was a business transaction, it was galling to be reminded of the fact. As though sensing my discomfort, Rolf seated himself beside me and laid his manicured hand over mine.

'My only regret is that I did not see you before the marriage agreement. If I had, I declare, I would have swept you off your feet and carried you to Scotland without staying for your grandsire's consent.'

My heart sang with joy. That I of all people should be so lucky. It was like reaching the end of the rainbow and finding gold. At that moment I was the most deliriously happy person in the whole world.

'You do me a great honour, sir . . . Rolf. I shall do my utmost to prove an obedient and dutiful wife.'

Rolf laughed. 'Come now. I'll require more than that. You must be my sweetheart; my mistress; my companion, but no simpering obedience, if you please. I receive a surfeit of that from the servants. I want a wife who is justly proud; who has a mind of her own and knows how to use it; who's capable of sharing my troubles and rejoicing in my joys. In short, I want a life's partner; a consort; a confidant with love in her heart.'

Smiling, I met his eyes. 'I trust I shall be all those things.' Then an imp of mischief prompted me to add: 'And I doubt if you'll be disappointed in my spirit.'

My words were greeted with a guffaw from Grandpa.

'Not if she proves to be a spark off me, but to business. The reason for intruding upon you in this unwarranted fashion. My letter telling her to stay the journey until the Hall is free of smallpox didn't reach her. So, not to mince matters, m'boy, she has arrived and has nowhere to stay. To have her at the Hall is to risk pocking her beauty, if not to gamble with her very life. So what shall we do, eh?'

There was silence in the great room and I blushed for the embarrassment of Rolf's position. It was unheard of for a young lady to thrust herself upon her fiancé in this manner.

Rolf removed his hand from mine and brushed some imaginary fluff from his knee. His answer when it came was light enough.

'Where should she stay but here? She will be well protected, you need have no anxiety on that score. It would be monstrously unfair for her to risk contracting the disease.'

The invitation sounded so sincere; so genuine, that I chided myself for having the fleeting impression that Rolf was not altogether pleased by the unexpected arrangement.

5

The next few hours were busy ones. Rolf, upon learning I had not eaten since breakfast, ordered a light meal of soup and chicken for me.

'It'll take the edge off your appetite until dinner.' Turning to Grandpa, he added, 'I trust you will honour us with your company this evening, sir?'

'Alack, no. The weather is unsuitable for night travel. In fact, I must take my leave if I'm to reach the Hall before dark.'

After Grandpa's departure Rolf introduced me to his housekeeper, Mrs. Dobbs. A plump, frizzy haired woman with a ready smile on her rosy face. I soon realized that her hearing was poor, though she managed well enough by reading the speaker's lip movements.

Once the introductions were made Rolf excused himself. 'Mrs. Dobbs will look after you. Have no hesitation in asking her for anything you need. I shall look forward to furthering our acquaintance at dinner.'

'Have you seen your room yet?' Mrs. Dobbs asked, when we were alone. 'The Master ordered the blue room for you. He keeps it for his special guests. It's in the west wing, next to his own, and has the advantage of the morning sun.'

I followed her up the wide oak staircase, with its dog-leg balusters; my feet noiseless on the thick red carpet. We turned left at the top and followed the balcony round to the far corner.

'Most of the guest rooms open off the staircase balcony. Mr. Mason—the butler,' she added, in reply to my questioning look, 'myself and the senior servants sleep in the east wing, the others in the attics. The men in the east wing and the women in the west.'

'Who uses the floor above this one?'

'No-one, except on special occasions, such as Grand Balls.'

'Do you have many such balls?' I asked, excited by the thought of being hostess on such gala occasions.

'Not these days. The last was to celebrate Mr. Rolf's wedding.'

'His wedding!' Her unexpected words shocked me.

'He's a widower. Didn't you know?'

The brilliance slipped from my happiness. It had not occurred to me that I was to be a second wife. Yet, it was hardly surprising. He was about ten years my senior, handsome and wealthy. Every mother with a marriageable daughter would be out to capture him. It was foolish to be disappointed; yet I was.

Mrs. Dobbs held open a panelled door and we stepped through into the west wing. On one side were four huge windows with red damask curtains looped against the jambs. Opposite them were four doors. Oak chests and cupboards stood against the walls and above them hung several portraits.

Mrs. Dobbs stopped before one of a delicate lady with golden hair. A dimpled smile hovered at the corner of her small mouth and her sapphire eyes regarded the viewer with frankness. There was something puzzlingly familar about the portrait. I looked inquiringly at Mrs. Dobbs.

'The master's first wife. We all adored her.'

'She looks charming,' I said, trying to quell the sprite of jealousy rising within me, but Mrs. Dobbs' next words unwittingly depressed me even more.

'She was the richest and most sought after young lady in society. We were all so proud the day she became Mistress of Marsh House.'

'Did she die in childbirth?' I asked, trying to feel some sympathy for my predecessor.

'No, poor love. That would have been bad enough, but this was far worse. She was shot.'

'Shot!' I looked again at the lovely serene face.

It was difficult to accept that so genteel a person could die so violently. In France during the revolution such happenings were commonplace, but not here in England.

Now I really did feel sympathy, both for her and for Rolf.

'Aye, five years ago, it was. Mr. Rolf was a great sportsman. One of the best marksmen for miles around, and we often housed shooting parties. The gentlemen loved the sport, but the mistress hated it. She was so tender hearted it grieved her to see the poor creatures hurt. He taught her to shoot, said it might save her life if Boney invaded us, and that shooting rabbits was good practice. She pretended to be a bad shot and used that as her excuse for never hitting anything. When the men were enjoying themselves, she would hide in the derelict cottage in the wood until the shoot was over. Rosie or I often slipped down to keep her company. It was a cruel trick of fate that neither of us were there the day she died.'

'You mean she died in the cottage?'

'Just outside. I was in bed with the ague at the time and Rosie was carrying a message to Captain Easy, but all the men heard her scream. They say she died before anyone reached her. The bullet hit her temple. Mr. Rolf was in the house at the time, awaiting an important messenger. He blamed himself for forcing her to go out with the shoot. Shut himself in the library for days and would speak with no-one but Mr. Mason. We feared for his sanity until Mr. Mason persuaded him to go away. That six months' holiday saved him. When he returned he put the past in its rightful place and took charge of his ships and estate once more, much to the relief of us all.'

'It must be dreadful to lose a loved one like that.'

'He never mentions her name now, so I wouldn't speak of her if I were you.'

'What of the person who shot her? It's a frightening thing to have such an accident on one's conscience.'

'Alack, that mystery was never solved. I suppose the guilty one took fright and lied. The suspicion still lingers over all who were at the shoot. The odd thing was all the gentlemen were carrying fowling-pieces, yet they say a bullet killed her.'

Now I could understand why Rolf was so willing to

take a bride he had never seen. Having lost the one woman he really loved, the business side of the bargain was more important than the loving. After such a dreadful tragedy, he deserved all the tenderness I could offer. In that instant I resolved that his happiness should be my prime mission in life.

The boudoir we entered was large, with two tulle covered windows stretching from the azure carpet to the pale blue ceiling. From each there was a magnificent view of the park. In the distance, towards the left, I could see the sails of brigs on their way south to London. Although my arrival two hours earlier had been totally unexpected, a fire now blazed in the grate and the room was cosily warm. Quite unlike my chamber of last night.

My box had been collected from the Dog and Partridge and was being unpacked by a maid whose dark hair was escaping from beneath her white mobcap. She was handling my shabby clothes with all the care she would have lavished on the finest silks.

'Rosie will maid you for the time being,' Mrs. Dobbs said, introducing us.

As the door closed behind the motherly housekeeper I felt embarrassed. I was accustomed to doing everything for myself and was therefore nonplussed as to what order to give the maid now hovering expectantly beside me. However, Rosie herself solved the problem.

'Shall I undo your hooks for you? Why not rest on the bed for half an hour. You must be tired after all your travelling.'

It was not until Rosie mentioned resting that I realized I was tired. Until that moment the excitement of seeing my future home and meeting Rolf had sustained me.

'An excellent idea,' I agreed, 'but don't allow me to sleep too long. I must look my best this evening.'

The girl's thoughtfulness impressed me. I was lucky to be surrounded by such kind people. As I closed my eyes I was ashamed of myself for feeling glad that I was staying here instead of at Grandpa's austere home.

The rest was refreshing and later I enjoyed the luxury of having a maid to help me dress. When I took a final look into the mirror I saw Rosie had worked wonders with my hair and the softened line was most becoming. My only regret was that my clothes were not more in keeping with the surroundings.

Mason greeted me at the foot of the stairs and led me to a small room on the opposite side to the library. I was surprised to find Rolf already entertaining two guests, for I had assumed we would be dining alone.

'Come in, my dear.'

Again I was aware of my good fortune in being affianced to one so handsome. He kissed my hand and drew me towards the fire.

'Gentlemen. Allow me to present my future wife, Miss Henrietta Debnam. Henrietta, my dear, this is Captain Easy and Captain Lloyd.'

Both were thick set, with gruff voices, and faces aged by seaspray. Captain Easy's hair was the colour of rosewood, while Captain Lloyd's was quite dark, and, like the sailors at the tavern, they were both wearing gold ear-rings. I learned from Rolf later of the fenmen's belief that wearing ear-rings aided one's eyesight.

It was disappointing that strangers were to be present during our first meal together, but I realized the fault rested with my unexpected arrival. Yet I was mystified by his choice of companions. They were the antitheses of himself, lacking his charm, grace, and poise.

For a while we sat sipping our glasses of Madeira wine, then Mason announced that dinner was served. We went through into the dining room beyond and sat at a long table, I at one end and Rolf at the other.

Though Rolf included me in the conversation, it soon became apparent that my presence was causing embarrassment, particularly towards the end of the meal when the wine loosened the captains' tongues and their remarks became bawdy.

At the earliest opportunity I excused myself and returned to my boudoir. Rosie, who was dozing in a chair by the fire, sprang to her feet to assist me to prepare for the night.

I was asleep almost from the moment my body sank into the luxurious softness of the feather bed, but my

43

dreams were haunted by images of the first Mrs. Cheval.

When I awoke Rosie was seated in the sunlight sewing.

'Mrs. Dobbs told me not to disturb you,' she said, when I exclaimed at the lateness of the hour. 'She said you were to be left to sleep your fill.'

Thoroughly refreshed, I threw back the covers and crossed to a window. The snow was reflecting its blue tinged brilliance across the fields; the birds chirped and sunbeams danced on the distant waves.

The sounds of horses turned my attention to the carriageway. I was surprised to see Rolf leaving in the company of his two captains, for I had not realized they were house-guests.

With Rosie's assistance I washed by the fire and dressed in my brown bodice and skirt. Mason was waiting in the vestibule.

'Good morning, Miss Debnam. I trust you slept well.'

'Excellently, thank you, Mason.'

As I spoke I realized how easy it was to accustom oneself to servants.

'Breakfast is usually served in here,' he said, opening the door to the ante-room I had passed through yesterday for my first meeting with Rolf.

The panelled walls made the room appear small. The sun, shining through the crested windows, threw jewelled coloured reflections onto the damask table cloth. An array of silver tureens stood on the large sideboard beside the library door.

'Mr. Cheval asked me to extend his apologies,' Mason said, as I helped myself to some ham and eggs. 'Urgent business commitments prevent him from attending you this morning but the stables and carriages are entirely at your disposal, should you wish to take the air. He hopes to return in time to dine with you this evening.'

The news was disappointing. As yet I had scarcely seen Rolf, except in the presence of others. Still, he was returning for dinner and that was something to anticipate.

A footman carried my plate to the table and Mason positioned my chair. The absurdity of not being allowed to do more for myself amused me.

The contrast of my life today with that of a fortnight ago was incredible. By this hour I would have collected the eggs, milked the goat and cow, fetched water from the well, cooked breakfast for my stepmother and probably already started churning the butter.

'What's your name?' I asked the footman, as he poured hot chocolate into my cup.

'The master prefers to call me Briggs, Madam.'

Though both servants remained in the room, it was a lonely meal, for neither spoke except to answer my questions. I was glad to return to my boudoir.

The bed was made and the tidied room had an untenanted appearance. For the first time in my life I was unsure how to occupy myself. The day stretched ahead endless and empty. My thoughts drifted to my recent travelling companion. I wondered what business had brought him to Marshsea in mid-winter. All our conversations had been on general topics or about myself and I knew nothing about his life. Not that it really mattered. We were unlikely to meet again. A fact which saddened me for I had never previously felt so content in another person's company.

Deciding I needed action, I tugged the tapestry bell ribbon. When Rosie appeared I gave orders for a horse to be saddled.

'As the morning is so agreeable,' I said, 'I shall explore Marshsea. It appears to be a delightful town.'

When I mounted some fifteen minutes later I realized a groom was expecting to accompany me.

'I prefer to ride alone,' I said.

'Begging your pardon, madam, but the master said I was to be certain to go with you, as you be a stranger in these parts.'

'I intend riding no further than the harbour. I shall not lose myself in so short a distance.'

Before he could reply I nudged the mare into a canter. It was not until I crossed the pack-bridge and paused to look at the ice covered dyke below, that I realized he was following me at a discreet distance. My instinct was to order him back to the house. Then I realized he was only doing his duty and I was flattered that Rolf should be so concerned for my safety. Providing the groom did not spoil my enjoyment of the crisp morning, he was welcome to follow.

The harbour was bustling with activity as the mare trotted along the path which cut the greensward in twain. It was a delightful scene. Pretty colour washed cottages nestled between cobble-stone ones. Fisherfolk chatted as their nets dried in the sun and their waiting boats bobbed against the old wall. In the harbour centre three brigs were surrounded by canal barges.

I paused to watch the whippers on the brigs jumping on and off their portable platforms, using their falling weight to haul the heavy baskets up from the hold. They were working in groups of four. Three clinging to a tail of the rope, while the fourth guided the swinging basket into position, then tipped its contents down the wooden shoot into the barge below. I noticed the bargemen worked fast to rake aside one load of coal before the next slithered down. Once a rope snapped. Instantly a child scaled the swaying yard-arm and pushed the free end back through the block fastened there. Work was resumed before the lad regained the deck. Up and down the men jumped, like puppets on strings.

My attention wandered to a group of children playing where the sea licked against the sand. They were laughing as they aimed pebbles at something in the water. I smiled, thinking how wise they were to enjoy themselves while they could for, by the time they were ten, they would be working like the youngster on the mast.

The tallest boy picked up a big stone and hurled it across the shimmering water. The answering howl as it hit its target drew my attention to the object of their aim.

It was a struggling puppy.

The creature's pitiful plight flooded me with rage. In an instant I had dismounted and was racing across the sands.

'How dare you?' I said, grasping the wrist of a boy about to throw another stone. 'You wicked, wicked, children.'

'It be only a stray.'

'Only a stray indeed. That puppy has as many feelings as you. How would you like to be out there in that freezing water with someone hurling stones at you?'

'Let me go. You hurt.' He wriggled to free himself.

'No more than you deserve.'

I was too angry to be aware of anything beyond my determination to stop the children continuing their cruel game. Not until the groom touched my arm did I notice that the swarthy fishermen were closing in a circle around me.

'You had better come away,' he advised.

Ignoring him, I turned back to the youngsters who were grinning insolently now their fathers were near.

'You deserve a good whipping, all of you.'

A burly man moved threateningly nearer. 'Lay a finger on him and yer'll get the leathering.'

There was a rumble of agreement. The colour rushed into my face as I turned towards the men.

'If these are your sons, then more is the shame on you for not teaching them right from wrong.'

'Are yer telling me what to do with me own kids?'

'Indeed I am. Their behaviour is a disgrace.'

They moved closer. I could smell the stench of fish on their clothes. Trying not to show my fear, I added:

'These children should be taught not to harm defence-less animals.'

'Go on, dad. Give her a wallop.'

The man raised his brawny arm, but before he could hit me, the groom lashed his riding whip down onto the man's wrist.

'You fools. Don't you know who she is?'

'Whoever she is she'll get something to remember. Aye, and you too. Nobody's going to meddle with our kids.'

'There be fast ways of dealing with busybodies,' agreed another. 'Let her have it, Fred.'

My arms were pinioned behind me.

'Stop, you fools.' There was fear in the groom's voice, but he faced them bravely. 'She's old man Hawkins grand-daughter. If you harm her, he'll have your hides for sails.'

The hands holding me dropped away. The man who

47

had been about to strike me paused, then lowered his arm. The crowd ebbed back. That one man's name should have such an intimidating effect on them made me even more angry.

'So, you're cowards into the bargain. Well, mark this. If I hear so much as a whisper of another animal being maltreated, whether by children or adults, I'll personally see they're justly punished. Now, one of you bring me that puppy.' I pointed to where the creature was struggling to gain a foothold on a mound of shingle edging the water. 'Handle it gently,' I added, as a child moved towards the sea, 'the stones have probably bruised it.'

As the boy came hesitantly forward, I took the bedraggled creature from him and handed it to the groom.

'Please hold it until I'm seated,' I said, then turning to my late adversary, I added, 'and you can assist me to mount.'

The subdued bully obediently followed me across the sands and cupped his hand for my foot. Once in the saddle I reached down for the puppy. As I tucked the trembling animal into the opening of my coat for warmth, a salt water stain spread over the velvet. Another time this would have dismayed me, but today my only concern was for the dog's comfort. Without a backward glance, I turned the mare towards Marsh House.

Mrs. Dobbs greeted me as I entered the vestibule.

'Oh, Miss Debnam, such excitement. The seamstress has arrived with material patterns for your new clothes. Mr. Hawkins has sent word that you're to have whatever you fancy. At least three day dresses and as many for the evening, not to mention coats and, of course, your wedding dress. Rosie and I've been counting the seconds until you returned.'

Earlier that morning I would have been equally excited, but now my only thought was for the puppy.

'That's indeed generous of him, but the matter must wait for the moment. Here's something decidedly more urgent.'

As I extricated it from its sanctuary it cringed against

me, fear showing in its black eyes. Its partially dried coat was a matted mess of sand and salt and it looked the oddest creature I had ever seen.

'Mercy gracious! Whatever is it?' Mrs. Dobbs exclaimed.

'A stray I rescued from the sea.'

'Poor little mite. One of the stable boys shall find it a home.'

'No. I shall keep it with me,' I said, filled with a desire to compensate it for the children's ill-treatment.

'Oh, my dear, that'll never do. Mr. Rolf's against animals living in the house.'

'Indeed,' I said, remembering that only yesterday Rolf had told me he wanted a spirited wife. 'Then this will be an exception. Please ask a maid to bring a bowl of water. The sooner he's bathed and dried the better.'

'I'll take him to the kitchen. A maid'll do it for you.'

'I prefer to do it myself,' I said, unwilling to add to the puppy's distress by handing him over to strangers. 'Pray see the water's sent to my boudoir immediately.'

I had expected one of the kitchen maids to bring it, instead Rosie entered, her face bright with excitement.

'Have you really rescued a puppy? Oh, isn't he sweet?'

I looked at him huddling in my arms.

'I'd hardly call him that at the moment, but he will be when he's clean. Please place the bowl on the rug by the fire. We must keep him as warm as possible.'

At first the water alarmed him but when he realized we meant no harm, he stood still obediently while we soaped his coat, then he shook himself, sending hissing spots into the fire.

When he was dry he returned my gaze dubiously, unable to believe his luck had changed.

'He must have a name,' I said. 'What shall it be?'

'Patch. What else with that black and white face, unless it be Loppy. He looks so funny with one ear standing up and the other hanging down. Lop-sided like.'

The puppy looked from one to the other, wanting to play but unsure if it dare.

'Patch it shall be,' I said, tickling his white head.

Contrary to my earlier expectations the day passed quickly. Patch became more adventurous with each passing hour and soon needed constant attention to keep him from mischief.

Mrs. Harris, the seamstress, had brought numerous patterns. She fluttered about my boudoir like a fussy hen, suggesting styles for each garment.

'You have such a perfect figure it will be a pleasure to dress you, madam,' she said.

Mrs. Dobbs and Rosie gained almost as much pleasure as me from making the selection. So it was with an aura of happiness that I joined Rolf that evening.

'There you are, my dear,' he said, rising to greet me. 'Come and sit by the fire and tell me why you're looking so pleased. I was afraid you'd find it dull without a companion.'

'Quite the contrary. It was a most exciting day. Have you not heard?'

'About your new clothes?'

He flicked the tails of his blue evening coat aside and sat so he could watch my face, making me glad I had given extra care to my appearance.

'I found a puppy.'

'Did you, by thunder, and here I was thinking that planning your new dresses had caused your eyes to sparkle so.'

'And I intend to keep it.'

He laughed. 'Why look so fierce? No-one is stopping you.'

Having expected him to oppose the notion, I was flummoxed by his reply.

'I was told you objected to animals in the house.'

'True, but it can live in the stables.'

'If it lives in the stables it'll not be my pet. I want it to live with me; wherever I am.'

The smile faded from his lips; his eyes hardened. I realized he was about to refuse my request.

'Please. I promise it will not annoy you in any way.'

For a moment he was silent, then his face relaxed.

'Very well, providing you understand I have no wish to see it. If it becomes a nuisance, out it will go.'

Dinner that evening was sumptuous compared to my fare at the farm, but I found the constant presence of Briggs and Mason inhibiting and knew it was an impediment I must overcome. In future there would always be servants present during meal-times. It was a relief when Rolf suggested that we should return to the anteroom.

'As there are no other guests here tonight, this will be more cosy than the library,' he said, seating himself beside me on the davenport.

Although we both did our best, the conversation remained strained and held none of the spontaneity which flowed so freely between Mr. Layton and myself.

Later as I lay in bed contemplating my first tête-à-tête with my fiancé I was dissappointed that the evening had been laborious. It was not Rolf's fault; his manner was impeccable. No-one could have been kinder; more considerate. Yet there remained an atmosphere of falseness; a restraint, as though each was aware of being on trial.

Grandpa's absence was the trouble. We needed his presence to bridge the gulf between us until we became better acquainted. I fell asleep wondering if Rolf was equally frustrated.

I cannot say how long I slept before being awakened by the clatter of a carriage arriving. Rolf had not mentioned that he was expecting guests, so I was puzzled as to who the nocturnal visitors might be. For a while I lay listening to the noises, then, as my insatiable curiosity overcame my manners, I pulled on my peignoir and crossed to the window.

The moonlight, reflected from the frozen snow, was bright but the portico roof hid the carriage from my view. Though I could not distinguish their words, the voices carried on the frosty air. One speaker was certainly Mason. Another possibly Rolf, but I could not be sure. One had a local brogue and several others spoke softly. Once a woman's laugh trilled and was hastily stifled.

Patch rubbed his cold nose against my ankle. I picked him up and was rewarded by a lick from his soft tongue.

Crossing to the mantelpiece, I lifted down the small

Dresden clock and read the time by firelight. Twenty past two. What possible reason could bring folk calling at such an hour? Had it been a stormy night I would have assumed a ship to be in distress, but there was not a breath of wind. Yet the callers must be unexpected or surely Rolf would have mentioned them, so who could they be unless . . .

Was it possible they had brought ill tidings from the Hall? Had Grandpa succumbed to the smallpox? Was he even now dying? Symptoms often developed quickly. Yet, surely it was not possible to be as hale as he appeared to be the day before yesterday and dangerously ill by tonight?

I wanted to hurry downstairs to assure myself all was well, but it would be bad manners for a guest to inquire the callers' business. There was nothing I could do but wait until someone came to my room.

I sat on the bed with Patch in my arms, every second expecting to hear the summoning knock. None came. The longer I waited, the more I magnified the possibility of Grandpa being ill. I told myself not to be foolish; that there was no cause for panic, but my imagination would not be appeased.

Half an hour later I could stand the tension no longer. Unconventional though it might be, I would have to go downstairs to assure myself everything was all right. With fumbling fingers I laid Patch back in his box at the foot of my bed and fastened the sash about my waist. Rolf's displeasure at my lack of manners could hardly be worse than the suspense of waiting for news.

I crossed to the door, turned the knob and pulled. It remained firmly closed. Thinking it to be jammed, I pulled again, harder this time. Still nothing happened. I tried a third time, then a fourth, rattling the knob in my determination to open the door. At last I was left with no alternative but to face the truth.

The door was locked from the outside. I was a prisoner in my own boudoir.

6

The fenmen's ways are strange, Mr. Layton had warned, yet surely even they did not lock guests in their rooms at night. My instinct was to pummel on the door until someone opened it, then I realized the futility of such action. For the first time I became aware of the room's remoteness. At this hour no-one would be in the kitchen to answer the bell and none of the servants were within calling distance. The younger ones were asleep in their attics two floors above. The older ones were ensconced in the east wing and separated from me by the width of the main house. The only solution was to wait until Rolf came to his room and then call to him and demand an explanation.

So I lit a candle and sat by the fire listening for his footsteps in the corridor. The voices on the portico ceased and the house became silent. The clock on the landing boomed the half hour, and then another before the voices sounded again. They were followed by the crunch of carriage wheels on the frozen snow. Hoping to learn more about the mysterious visitors, I crossed to the window, but it was a closed carriage below. The only person visible was the driver seated high on his box in the moonlight.

There were no more logs for the fire and the room was becoming chilly. The clock boomed again. To overcome the cold I lay on the bed under the goose feather quilt and, although I was determined to remain awake, I did not hear the clock strike four-thirty.

Next morning the fire was blazing and Patch missing from his box as I jumped from the bed. The door opened easily. Puzzled I tested it for any inclination to stick. It moved quite freely. Though I searched, I could find no key. I stepped into the corridor, half expecting it to look different in some way, but it was as serene as yesterday.

As I stood gazing at the beautifully carved chests and cupboards standing against the walls, Rosie came up the servants' staircase carrying Patch.

'Did you wonder where he was?' she asked, standing him on the carpet so he could run to greet me. 'I thought it wisest to take him out early. I tried not to disturb you.'

Patch bounced on his hind legs, tapping with his front paws against the crumped skirt of my peignoir. I lifted him up and carried him into the room.

'Why was my door locked last night?' I asked.

Rosie looked startled. 'What an odd question. Why ever would anyone want to lock it?'

'Presumably to prevent me from leaving this room, but why?'

'Maybe it just stuck, wood often swells in winter. Yes, that must be what happened, for it was certainly not locked this morning.'

'It opens easily enough now. Wood does not swell and shrink again that quickly. Not without good cause.'

Rosie poured my washing water into the china bowl. 'Perhaps you had a touch of the nightfrights. Sometimes those horrid dreams are so real a body is sure they happened.'

Had I not been wearing my peignoir when I awoke, Rosie's suggestion might have been feasible. However, there was little point in pursuing the subject with her, but I was determined to mention it to Rolf for, whoever had locked the door, had unfastened it again while I slept. Meanwhile there was still the other mystery.

'Who came here last night?' I asked.

Rosie looked at me sharply. 'No-one.'

'Several people came in a carriage and four. They arrived about two-thirty.'

'If anyone had, the maids would have been roused to attend them. If you ask me, you had a right bad touch of the nightfrights. I dream the house is afire and we're trapped in the attics. It seems so real I wake all of a heat, only to find nothing has happened. Everyone but me is asleep.'

As I dressed I puzzled over the night's activities. Whatever Rosie said I was convinced that something odd had happened at Marsh House last night.

Rolf was already in the breakfast room when I entered. Immediately our greetings were over I put the question uppermost in my mind.

'Why was I locked in my boudoir last night?'

His expression was one of incredulity.

'My dear Henrietta, what an absurd notion. I can assure you no-one would do such a thing. What an extraordinary idea.'

His answer was bewildering. 'Then may I have the key to it?' I asked, half expecting a refusal.

'Certainly if you wish, though I fail to see the necessity. However, if you want it, you must see Mrs. Dobbs, the matter is her concern, not mine. She'll doubtless find you one.'

Now I was even more puzzled. If he had not ordered the locking of my door, then who had? I glanced at Mason. He had overheard our conversation, yet his impassive face showed no trace of interest. Remembering the nocturnal arrival of the carriage, I asked if the other guests were breakfasting in their rooms.

'I see the table is laid only for ourselves,' I added.

'There are no other guests.'

'So the coach did bring a message then,' I said. 'I wondered if it had, as it was such a late hour to arrive. I was frightened it might be news that Grandpa had caught the smallpox.'

'No-one came here last night.'

'But they did. I saw them.'

Rolf's eyes hardened as he dabbed the corner of his mouth with the napkin. 'If this is some kind of tease I must inform you I'm never in the humour for jesting at this hour. Frivolities are best reserved for the evening's entertainment.'

'I'm not jesting.'

'I trust you are,' he said, with a coldness in his voice I had not previously heard. 'It would not please me to discover my future wife's given to a fanciful imagination. I've had one such and have little mind for another to be thrust upon me.'

My cheeks reddened at the humiliating comment. 'I'm indeed sorry to hear you consider me to be thrust upon you. I assure you the wish was not mine. You at least were party to the agreement. My opinion was never consulted.'

For a moment we stared angrily at each other, then he leaned across the table and covered my hand with his.

'Forgive me, my dear. It was a slip of the tongue and not meant in the way it may have sounded. Can I hope for your pardon?'

My temper was still ripe but to quarrel so early in our relationship would not pave the way to future happiness. Also I was anxious to know why he called his first wife fanciful. Had she too been locked in her room; heard mysterious carriages arrive during the night. I forced a smile.

'Certainly . . . and please accept an apology for my retort.'

He touched my cheek with the tip of his elegant fingers.

'You're even more comely when the rage is on you. I like a woman with spirit. A timid filly is good for no one. Today I intend calling upon your grandsire. I shall suggest to him that the wedding date be advanced. As you're living in my house anyway, there's little reason for delaying the ceremony. Will a fortnight from today suit you?'

'So soon?'

'Don't you approve of the suggestion?'

I hesitated. As he said, there was no reason for delay. The agreement was signed; arrangements made. There was no man I would rather marry; no-one my heart yearned to please. As Rolf's wife I would have everything. Fine clothes; jewellery; an assured place in society. I should indeed be grateful to Grandpa for arranging such an admirable match, yet. . . .

'I had hoped we might become better acquainted first.'

'We shall have a fortnight. Is that not more than sufficient? Come, what say you?'

A tap at the door spared the necessity of a reply. A maid entered and handed Mason a letter. He placed it on a silver salver and carried it to me.

Rolf smiled at my surprise. 'Probably your Grandsire inquiring after your health.'

'This is not his handwriting, nor his seal,' I replied, puzzled by the fact the letter bore no post mark.

I broke the seal and smoothed the sheets of cream parchment. The message, written in capital letters, was brief and unsigned.

'IF YOU VALUE YOUR LIFE DO NOT MARRY ROLF CHEVAL.'

He noticed my swift intake of breath. 'What is it, my dear? The contents appear to disturb you.'

'Nothing. Nothing at all.'

Though I tried to assume a pretence that the letter was unimportant, my eyes continued to stare at the cryptic message.

'May I see it?'

'No, please . . . it's personal,' I said, not wishing to embarrass him.

I folded the letter, intending to slip it into my pocket but he stopped me.

'I insist. I cannot permit my fiancée to have secrets from me.'

'It's addressed to me. You've no right to read it.'

His hand closed over mine. 'As your future husband I have every right. Kindly hand it to me.'

'No.'

The twist he gave my arm caused pain to shoot to my shoulder. The letter dropped to the table.

'That was unforgiveable,' I said, aghast at the unexpected ruthlessness of the man I was due to marry.

'Possibly, but I'm not in the habit of allowing my requests to be balked.'

He frowned as he read the crude message.

'Who wrote this? By the devil, he shall rue it. Who

was it? Some love lorn suitor? If you think you can deceive me. . . .'

'I know no-one in the district, except Grandpa. You can hardly accuse him of sending it.'

'What of the damned fellow who squired you to the Hall when you arrived? Are you not acquainted with him?'

Rolf's lack of trust in my honesty annoyed me more than the pain to my wrist.

'That notion is absurd, as well you know. Mr. Layton was a mere travelling companion who did me a kindness. A chance acquaintance I'm not likely to meet again. Besides, he thinks I'm living at the Hall. Perhaps you should question your servants. They will presumably know who delivered it.'

While we waited for Mason to come back I pretended to eat my breakfast, but my appetite had vanished. Not only was I unable to comprehend why anyone should send me such a disquieting message, but I was also seeing a new side of Rolf's character. His black eyebrows were drawn together over the bridge of his Roman nose and his lips were pressed into a hard line. It was an angry, cruel expression. Briggs, standing motionlessly behind his master's chair, was watching us warily. I was glad when Mason returned.

'There's little to tell, sir. The scullery maid found it by the kitchen doorstep. Anyone could have placed it there.'

'Surely someone saw a messenger approaching the house? Why do I pay you if it's not to protect us?'

'Normally they would, sir, but the sea mist is dense this morning A messenger could come within feet of the house and not be noticed.'

Rolf pushed his chair back, screwed the letter into a ball and threw it into the fire.

'In future all letters addressed to Miss Debnam are to be brought to me. She must not be bothered by such nonsense.'

The order increased my annoyance. 'If I should receive more such letters I'm quite capable of ignoring them.'

'You must allow me to judge what is good for you.

I know more of worldly matters. Now I must be on my way, there's a busy day ahead. Take care of yourself until I return.'

To my surprise he dropped a light kiss on my forehead. It was the first kiss of any kind that I had received from him and the fact that he chose that moment to bestow it irritated me.

I was unlikely to receive letters from anyone, except possibly Grandpa, for my step-mother would not bother with such trivialities and dear old Daniel could not write. Even so, it was presumptuous of Rolf to insist upon scrutinising my correspondence. I was not yet his wife.

My cheeks burned with anger as I climbed the stairs. The letter was probably written by a vicious person with a grudge against Rolf, but that did not excuse Rolf's manner towards me.

In the corridor I stopped before the portrait of the first Mrs. Cheval. Had she been happy or afraid of him? Mrs. Dobbs had described her as gentle; Rolf had called her fanciful. It occurred to me that she too might have received anonymous letters. If they had distressed her, it might account for Rolf's insistence upon vetting my correspondence. Perhaps he had not yet realized that I was of different fibre. It would take more than a few such letters to influence my judgement.

When I entered the boudoir Rosie was sewing a ribbon more securely to my calash. Patch rose from the rug, his tail wagging so fast he toppled over. I lifted him up and tickled his tummy.

'Has he behaved himself?'

'He whimpered a little after you left, then settled and went to sleep.'

I noticed her gentle voice was unmarred by the long vowels common to the other servants. To help to cool my anger I asked:

'Have you always lived in these parts?'

'No, my home was in London. I came with Mrs. Elaine when she married the master. I was her personal maid. My mother was her mother's maid and we played together as children, so it was only natural that I should take care of her when she grew up.'

'You were very fond of her?'

'She was the sweetest creature that ever lived. So kind and gentle. Everyone loved her. She should never have come here. This was not the life for her, not shut up here in this great house with only me for company.'

'She had her husband too.'

'Aye, she had him.'

'You sound disapproving. Were they not happy?'

Rosie shrugged. 'His ways were not hers.'

'How so? He is a most handsome gentleman.'

Rosie's needle flashed betwixt the ribbon and velvet. The china clock ticked and the fire spluttered.

'Come, you have not answered my question.'

'As you say, he's a handsome gentleman.'

'But you do not approve of him?'

'A servant has no right to approve or disapprove, though it is often hard to stand by and say nothing. She needed someone to cherish her; make her happy; spoil her a little.'

'And he did none of these things?'

The nicest part of me was sorry that she had not been happy at Marsh House. Yet, although I knew it was unkind, I was relieved that the marriage had not been idyllic for it gave me a better chance of winning his love.

At breakfast he had commented on her fanciful imagination, now Rosie was referring to her as needing cosseting. Had she, in fact, behaved like a spoilt child? I felt I had to learn more about her.

'What was she like?' I asked. 'You said she was kind and gentle, was she also imaginative?'

'If you mean did she see the ghost, yes she did, and if Miss Elaine said she did, you can depend upon it, she did.'

The unexpectedness of Rosie's reply startled me.

'I didn't know there was one. Have you seen it?'

'No, but I know it exists. Miss Debnam, may I give you a mite of advice? Don't pry into things which are not your concern.'

Rosie looked so intense I expected the slender needle to snap between her thin fingers.

'Are you suggesting something is wrong?'

Her eyes faltered and dropped to the sewing. 'No . . . I . . . was just meaning supernatural things . . . ghosts and the like.'

She spoke hesitantly, as though regretting the warning. I received the impression that, whatever Rosie really meant, it had little to do with ghosts, but it was obvious from her now fast moving needle that it would be useless to pursue the matter at the moment.

I moved to the window and noticed the sunlight was trying to penetrate the low mist. Patch squiggled in my arms; his cheeky eyes regarding me hopefully.

'He wants to walk,' I said, rubbing my nose against his silky head. 'The fog is lifting now and the exercise will be good for us both. Please fetch my boots.'

'Do you think it wise? The mist could come down again fast. Let me take him.'

'Have no fear. I shall not venture far enough to lose my way.'

Though Rosie was dubious about the wisdom of the proposed walk, Patch's desire for it was obvious. He scampered about the room picking up everything he could carry. Then he tugged at my bootlaces as Rosie tried to tie them.

'Come here, you rogue,' I said, lifting him out of her way. 'Nobody needs your help.'

He wagged his stumpy tail and tried to lick my nose. When I opened the door he raced along the corridor and down the stairs. Near the bottom he lost his balance and tumbled the last two steps, landing in an undignified ball at Mason's feet. The butler's disdainful glance moved from Patch to me.

'I was not informed of your wish to go out, madam, but the carriage shall be made ready immediately.

'Thank you, Mason, but I intend walking to exercise this young rascal.'

'Briggs will do that for you, madam.'

'I prefer to do it myself.'

'Then I will call him to accompany you.'

'That is not necessary,' I replied, pulling on my gloves

as I crossed the vestibule. 'I've no intention of going far.'

Mason opened the storm door reluctantly. 'It's most unwise to venture forth alone on a morning like this. The master will not approve.'

Without replying I fastened the velvet collar higher about my neck and followed Patch down the portico steps.

The weather had changed during the night. The crisp coldness was replaced by a dribbling dankness, which penetrated my clothes. Fortunately my calash offered perfect protection against the melting snow trickling from the lime trees edging the carriageway. Occasionally shafts of sunlight perforated the gloom. Yet, though it brought a ray of colour to the surrounding greyness, it added no warmth.

I threw a stick for Patch who fetched it gleefully, then refused to relinquish it. I scolded him and gently forced open his jaws. Soon he learned what was required and obediently dropped it for another throw, but the coldness was hostile. I decided to run to warm myself. Patch showed his approval by bounding round my legs; at times almost tripping me up. We crossed the pack-bridge and raced laughing and barking down the far side. A passing horseman emerged from the mist, called the morning greeting and disappeared again.

At last I could run no further. Patch, wanting the game to continue, tugged at my coat.

'That's naughty,' I admonished, tapping his black nose. After the third reproving tap he regarded me quizzically; his head coquettishly askew. I threw another stick. Instantly he was after it. Then something in the bedraggled hedgerow caught his attention. As he investigated a beautiful cock pheasant rose and skimmed low over the road, its green and brown plumage adding a welcome splash of colour to the grey day. Patch dropped the twig and bounded after the bird. At the same moment the mist swirled thicker, blotting out all visibility.

'Patch, come back, Patch. Patch.'

Too late I realized the danger. Even without the disadvantage of the mist, Patch would not know the way back to his new home. I chided myself for not finding a collar and leash before starting out. As I raced forward, the fog ebbed sufficiently for me to see him squeeze under a gate.

'Patch, come back you naughty boy,' I cried, as he again merged with the mist.

The moss covered wood smeared my coat as I climbed the gate. Fortunately the imprint of his paws showed clearly on the snow. Trees appeared like ghosts as I raced after him. Once I almost collided with a windmill, its great sails useless without the wind. The snow gave way to soggy bracken and tracking became more difficult.

'Patch, where are you?'

I ran on, heedless of the direction. Though he had been my pet for only a day, he was already precious. He was so friendly and trusting. It was horrifying to think he might be maltreated again; killed even. I chided myself for allowing him to run free in the fog.

I caught a glimpse of him, then the mist closed again and there was nothing but his bark to guide me. A wide dyke blocked my way. His bark came challengingly from the far side of the ice. A bridge. There must be a bridge; a plank; anything by which I could cross the ice. Frantically I ran in one direction, then the other, but there was nothing. I remembered the skaters I had seen gliding over the dykes during my journey from Cambridge, but that was before the thaw started. Would it hold my weight now?

I took a firm grip of some bracken and lowered my foot onto the ice. It held firm. Warily, ready to swing back instantly, I transferred all my weight to that leg. The ice remained hard. I released my hold of the bracken and moved cautiously forward, testing each step before adding my weight. My courage increased as I progressed towards the centre.

The fog swirled away in one of its periodic clearances and I saw Patch standing on the opposite bank. So great was my relief that I forgot my danger. All my attention was on the nearness of capture.

Crack!

The noise came without warning. It was instantly

followed by several others. As the ice broke I flung myself towards the nearest bank, but it was out of reach. Black water oozed through the hole, greedily sucking at my boot. I grabbed at the ice, trying to find something, anything to serve as a hand hold. There was nothing.

'Help. For mercy sake, help me.'

Even as I shouted I knew it was hopeless. During the entire outing I had passed only one other person. Patch, sensing my panic, began to whimper. The freezing water was numbing my body; the weight of my sodden clothes pulling me downwards. My fingers lost their sense of feeling as I fought for survival. It was only a matter of time, before I was dragged beneath the ice. Once under, death was certain. Somehow I must keep my head above water.

The sun peeped mockingly through the mist. It was a silent morning. No birds sang, no gulls swooped for food. Only my screams and Patch's whimpering broke the stillness.

Then I heard something else. A sound so faint I thought it an hallucination, but the galloping hooves came nearer.

'Help,' I shouted. 'For mercy sake, help me.'

For a terrifying second I thought the rider had not heard and would pass by. Then came an answering shout.

'What's the trouble? Where are you?'

'Here. In the dyke. I've fallen through the ice.'

'Haven't you more sense than to walk on ice when it's thawing? Keep calling. I need your voice to guide me.'

'Hurry. Please hurry.'

The horse appeared on the bank and the rider slid from its back.

'You!'

We spoke in unison.

'Hold on,' Mr. Layton added. 'I need something for a life-line.' He unfastened the bridle and flung one end towards me. 'Catch this. I'll try to pull you towards me.'

I wound the strap round my hand, for my fingers were

64

no longer capable of retaining a grip. Never will anything seem as blessed as that strip of leather.

'Of all the damn fool things to do,' he said, when I was at last near enough to reach his outstretched hand. 'You might have been drowned. It's nothing but a miracle that I happened along,' he added, hauling me to the bank.

The reprimand mixed with the relief of finding myself once more standing on firm ground, was too much for my control. Tears rolled unchecked down my face.

'I was trying to reach my puppy.'

His arms closed comfortingly about me. 'Don't cry. You're safe now.'

He was speaking soothingly, as though to a frightened child. He wiped away the tears and gently kissed my forehead.

'Your life is far more precious than that of any puppy.'

'I'm sorry to be such a fool,' I said, looking up at him.

Then, without my realizing how it happened, his lips were on mine; his arms crushingly tight about me. The kiss ended as abruptly as it began and he pushed me away.

'Here, wrap this around you,' he said, taking off his top coat.

I looked at him wonderingly, but his face was expressionless as he added:

'Come on, up on Bess with you. She'll carry us both the short distance to Marshsea.'

'But my dog.'

'I'll see to him. You just do as I tell you,' he ordered.

7

Instead of going to the tavern Mr. Layton stopped outside a stone cottage by the harbour.

'I've leased it for a month or two,' he explained.

The indiscretion of entering such a dwelling accompanied by a gentleman was forgotten in my need for warmth. As I crouched beside the fire blazing on the brick hearth Patch, who had come to heel willingly at Mr. Layton's command, nuzzled against my leg.

Mr. Layton crossed to the adjoining room and returned with a thick dressing-robe and a coarse towel.

'Take off your wet clothes and put that on,' he commanded.

'I can't do that,' I said, appalled by the impropriety of such an action, particularly after the impetuous way he had kissed me.

'Don't be doltish. The one thing you can't do is remain in those soaked clothes. I've no intention of molesting you if that's what you fear. You'll have ample time to change while I go to the pump on the square for some drinking water.'

After he left I checked that the window shutters were closed and, before taking off my saturated clothes, I bolted the door against possible intruders.

A brisk rub with the scratchy towel restored my circulation and brought a glow to my limbs. When Mr. Layton returned, I was comfortably wrapped in his robe, with the sleeves turned back to a manageable length.

I was embarrassed by my clothes hanging round the fire, but it was the only way to dry them quickly. Mr. Layton nodded his approval.

'You're already looking better. I'll make you a hot toddy, then I'll ride to Marsh House for some dry clothes.'

66

'How do you know I'm living there?' I asked, remembering the anonymous letter.

'Secrets are not easily kept in these parts.'

He bailed some water out of the pail and poured it into the kettle.

'But how?'

'Yesterday you were out riding with one of the Cheval grooms . . . at least, the fishermen said he was from Marsh House.'

'In that case I suppose you also know about the dispute on the beach. Are the local people very angry with me?'

'Quite the contrary.' He swung the heavy iron kettle over the fire. 'Your action in defending the puppy against a hostile crowd, especially one led by the local bully, gained you their admiration. The one thing the fenmen value above others, is courage.'

'I acted without thinking. It was a foolhardy thing to do, but I could not stand aside watching them stone Patch.'

'Foolhardy or not, they are proud of you. They regretted that old Silas had no male heir to carry on the business and were fearful for their livelihood. Now they say that, you may be only a lass, but you are a true splinter off the old spar.'

His assurance thrilled me. More than anything I wanted to be liked by the local people. I was glad that my impulsive action had not condemned me in their eyes.

As the blackened kettle began to sing a contentment filled me and I found myself telling him about the letter.

'Mr. Cheval suggested you wrote it,' I added, watching his face for any sign of guilt.

'Then Mr. Cheval's grossly mistaken. It's not my way to send unsigned letters, particularly ones likely to distress a lady. That is a shameful action.'

'Have you any idea who might have written it? Could it be someone who was on the beach yesterday?'

'I doubt it. Most of them cannot write. There was little

67

learning for children in these parts until your grandfather helped Mrs. Wyatt to start her day school.'

'Then who could it be! What has Mr. Cheval done that someone should think it necessary to warn me against him?'

Mr. Layton took the kettle from the fire and poured hot water onto the whisky. 'Rich men have enemies,' he said. 'Someone chose this way to annoy him. In my opinion he was wise to insist upon scrutinizing your correspondence. Anonymous letters are written by deranged people, and can be most unpleasant. Drink this as hot as possible,' he added, 'it'll help to prevent a chill.'

'You know nothing against him then?'

It was wrong of me to ask such questions but a seed of doubt had entered my thoughts. I wanted someone to tell me that Rolf was as perfect as I hoped.

'I have not the honour of the gentleman's acquaintance. Do you mind waiting alone while I ride to Marsh House?'

'Don't go,' I said hastily, 'I mean, I would rather no-one else learned of my foolishness. The servants warned me of the dangers of walking alone. It would be embarrassing to admit them right. My clothes are drying rapidly. In an hour they will be fit to wear. It would take almost as long to fetch others.'

We sat one each side of the blazing fire with Patch sleeping on the floor between us. Just like a married couple, I thought, watching the firelight glow on his face. He was not as handsome as Rolf, but his countenance was friendly; the kind which invites confidences. I felt remarkable happy and relaxed in his company as I asked about the cottage.

'I acquired it quite by chance,' he replied. 'After escorting you to the Hall, I came here to watch the brigs being unloaded and one of the fishermen mentioned it. The old lady who lives here has gone to stay with her daughter, so I was able to rent it for a few weeks. It's more convenient that living at the tavern.'

'You intend staying then?'

The thought of him remaining in the neighbourhood was unaccountably pleasing.

'For the time being, yes.'

'On business?'

'More a kind of holiday. I was wounded in Spain. Nothing much, but the physician suggested that the bracing air would speed my recovery.'

'So you're a soldier,' I said, hoping to learn more about him.

'Major in the dragoons, but while I am here I prefer to be known as plain Mister.'

'As you please, though many would gladly shake the hand of any gentleman who fought those barbarous Frenchmen.'

We lapsed into silence, each satisfied to sit gazing at the flames. I was tempted to mention the mystery of my locked door, but decided against it. In this cosy room, with Patch's gentle snores, the suggestion that someone was keeping me prisoner at night seemed ludicrous. Particularly as Rolf was willing for me to have the key.

Time passed serenely. I should have felt embarrassed relaxing there with only Mr. Layton's dressing-robe to cover my nakedness. Instead I was filled with a deep contentment.

When my clothes were dry Mr. Layton went to fetch the horse while I dressed cosily by the fire. The mist was swirling thickly as he helped me to mount Bess and handed Patch up to me. He walked beside the mare as far as the park gates.

'It might be best for you to walk from here,' he said. 'That way your return will cause little comment.'

He held Patch while I slid to the ground. 'I am greatly in your debt,' I said, taking Patch from him. 'If there is ever anything I can do for you, I shall be only too delighted.'

It was with a sense of loss that I watched him mount Bess and merge with the mist. Patch struggled to be free, and I tightened my hold of him as I hurried to the house. Mason met us at the storm door, for once looking harassed.

'There you are, madam. The entire household is in

69

a turmoil. All the male servants are scouring the countryside. We were of the opinion something dire had befallen you.'

The colour flushed my cheeks. It had not occurred to me that the servants might become alarmed by my absence, for at the farm, I was used to absolute freedom. No-one there cared whether or not I returned from an expedition.

'My apologies. It was thoughtless of me to cause anxiety, but as you see, I'm quite safe.'

'It is nigh on four of the clock. The seamstress has been waiting these last three hours.'

Though Mason spoke politely I felt like an errant child. The knowledge that I deserved a reprimand sharpened my voice.

'Then she must continue waiting until I have tidied myself. Kindly send Rosie to me,' I said, mounting the stairs.

On looking in the boudoir mirror I was shocked by my appearance and wondered if Mason guessed a mishap had occurred. My velvet coat, still slightly damp, clung about me and great, slimy, brown stains disfigured the skirt. To add to my chagrin, my little pansy brooch was missing. Its loss was particularly distressing, for it had been a present from old Daniel and I prized it as a keepsake. Now it was probably lying at the bottom of the dyke; where I might have been had not Mr. Layton happened along at the crucial moment.

When Rosie entered I noticed that she had been crying and I felt a fresh twinge of guilt.

'Oh, Miss Debnam. I am that glad to see you. We thought something terrible had happened.'

'Nonsense. What could happen? I . . . I . . . just went a little further than I intended, that's all.'

'A body hears of such dreadful accidents. Folk falling into the harbour or bowled over by carriages, and there are so many soldiers about, I declare, it's not safe for a maid to walk alone, even on a fine day.'

'You thought I might have met a fate worse than death?' I joked, trying to make light of her fears. 'This is the nineteenth century, not the dark ages.'

'Only last year Captain Peacock's daughter vanished because she would go walking alone. They say the white slavers got her.'

'I should think a lover more likely. As you can see, I'm quite safe.'

'But your coat. It wouldn't be worse if you'd fallen into a dyke.'

'The fog is damp. Pray see that a maid cleans it for me. I'll need to wear it until my new one is ready.'

Rosie helped me to change into fresh clothes, then brushed my hair into another chignon. I waited by the fire while she went to fetch the seamstress.

Mrs. Dobbs returned with them and, although her greeting was polite, I knew she was angry with me. I wondered if Rolf would be told of my escapade, but decided it unlikely. None of the servants would be anxious to admit allowing me to walk alone in the fog.

'You wish to see me?' I asked, turning to Mrs. Harris. 'Is there some difficulty regarding my choice of materials?'

'No, madam. Your wedding dress is ready for a fitting.'

'So soon? But that's impossible.'

'Me and the girls worked most of the night. Mr. Cheval said you would need it almost immediately,' she replied, placing the wicker valise on the davenport.

The news annoyed me. Considering Grandpa was paying for my clothes, Rolf had no right to interfere. A day gown or coat was of far greater priority but, as the dress was reverently lifted from its wrapping, I gasped with delight. Even in this unfinished state it looked exquisite. It was made from the finest peach silk, with a plunging neckline both back and front, the opening being filled with spring green lace. It fastened high under the chin in the mode once favoured by the Tudors. At the back the frills rippled down to the hem.

'Oh, Miss Debnam, you will look a proper picture in that,' Rosie exclaimed. 'Do try it on.'

When the bodice was fastened I stood back to view myself in the long gilt mirror.

'I declare you are pretty as a fairy,' Rosie said. 'Your

hair must be taken up so.' She pinned it high on my head, and allowed two ringlets to fall to my shoulders. 'We can fasten it with a posy of matching rose buds, if Mrs. Harris will make one for us.'

'Why bless you, yes, Miss. Only too pleased to be sure.'

My reflection was certainly gratifying, yet I lacked the glow of happiness which ought to accompany such an occasion. Rolf would gladden any bride's heart, yet the idea of hastening the wedding frightened me. Until today it had been a distant event; a host of tomorrows away. Trying on the dress made me realize that my days of freedom were severly limited.

The others were surprised by the speed with which I concluded the fitting.

'Is something troubling you?' Rosie asked, as the door closed behind the older women. 'Are you feeling poorly?'

'I'm just a little weary,' I said, lying on the bed. 'Please draw the bed curtains. I wish to rest a little before dinner.'

Within minutes I was asleep, but not at peace. My dreams were haunted by the wedding dress. First I was walking up the aisle wearing it, but, however fast I walked, I could not reach the groom. Then I was in Mr. Layton's cottage with the dress all ragged and torn and could see Rolf peering through the window.

I awoke unrested, to find the candles relit, and Rosie standing by the bed.

'The master's sent word that he'll not be home for dinner,' she said, placing my spare dress in readiness.

The news was disappointing, although making conversation with Rolf was not the easiest of occupations.

However, the evening was not uneventful. The meal was almost over when Mason was summoned from the dining room. He returned a few minutes later looking somewhat hesitant.

'A gentleman is at the door, madam. He insists upon speaking with you.'

'A messenger from Mr. Hawkins you mean?'

'I think not. He's a military gentleman and says the

matter's most urgent. I told him you were at dinner, but he was insistent; most insistent. His card, madam.'

My heart beat quickened. Mr. Layton was the only military gentleman I knew, but my hopes were dashed as I read the card

'I cannot recall knowing a Lieutenant Stubbs. Is he a friend of Mr. Cheval?'

'Not to my knowledge, madam. He asked first for the master then, upon learning he was not at home, he asked to see you.'

'By name?'

'Yes, madam.'

Mason looked as puzzled as I felt.

'If we are to learn his business, I suppose I must see him. Pray show him into the ante-room, I will receive him there and Mason, in the circumstances, I think it might be as well if you remained in the room with us.'

For once Mason's smile was almost friendly. 'Certainly, if that is your wish, madam.'

The man was tall, thick set and wearing a red and black militia uniform.

'Your servant, ma'am.'

The heels of his black boots clicked as he bowed.

'I don't think I have the pleasure of your acquaintance, Lieutenant,' I said.

'We met once before, ma'am. I was the officer who stopped your coach the evening you arrived in Marshsea.'

'Indeed? So it's you I have to thank for frightening the wits from me. I thought you to be highwaymen.'

'It was not our intention to alarm you, ma'am. That's the last thing I, or indeed any of my men, would wish. We're here to guard your safety.'

'Is that the reason for tonight's visit?'

'In a way, yes. It concerns the Frenchies who escaped last week. Earlier this evening we sighted them down by the harbour. Having received warning of their plans to cross tonight, we were waiting for them. Shots were fired, but, it being such a foul night, they escaped in the darkness. Yet we think one of them received a bullet. In which case their travels will be hampered. The town is surrounded. They'll not find escaping from here as easy as from Norman's Cross.'

'I fail to see how this concerns either Mr. Cheval or myself.'

'Like all trapped vermin, ma'am, they are dangerous and need food and shelter. A remote house like this would be ideal for them. So I've come to warn you to bar your doors and shutter the windows. They have pistols and are not afraid to use them.'

'I'm sure I can rely on Mr. Mason to see that we're adequately protected, is that not so?' I asked.

The butler moved closer to my chair. 'Most certainly, madam.'

The Lieutenant nodded his approval. 'The streets'll be dangerous tonight,' he added. 'May I suggest it wisest if no-one ventures out?'

'Unfortunately Mr. Cheval's not home yet.' I glanced at Mason. 'Is there any way for us to warn him of the danger?'

'I fear not, madam, but there's little cause for alarm. He's gone to Lynn and will return along the top road.'

'Then pray be kind enough to warn the servants. As for myself,' I added, turning to the Lieutenant, 'I assure you I've no intention of deserting the house in this weather.'

The Lieutenant clicked his heels.

'Then I'll take my leave, ma'am, but there's one more thing before I go. We know from our intelligences that a black haired lady's assisting their escape.'

My hand moved instinctively to my hair.

'Then I assure you it's not I. Good night, Lieutenant. We're obliged to you for the warning.'

As the door closed behind him I wondered if Mr. Layton knew of the danger. The earlier shooting probably took place near his cottage and the possibility that he might be involved, however innocently, was disturbing. I knew it was foolish to concern myself about him, yet he was constantly in my thoughts.

A few minutes after I entered my boudoir Rosie came in carrying Patch.

'He's just had his run,' she said. 'Mr. Mason insisted

74

that Briggs and John took him. He said I was not to set foot outside the house tonight. I hope I did right in letting him go with them, but Mr. Mason was so insistent.'

'Yes, of course. The militia have warned us not to go out. They think those horrid French prisoners are at last cornered.'

Rosie helped me to undress, then went to her own room. For a while I played with Patch then, feeling weary, I extinguished the candles. It was not until I was in bed that I remembered I had not asked Mrs. Dobbs for the boudoir key. I contemplated ringing for Rosie, then I realized that she would not hear the bell from her attic room. If I wanted the key I must go to Mrs. Dobbs' room myself, but the bed was enticing and the thought of negotiating the dim and draughty corridors repulsive. Tomorrow would do equally well.

At first I was determined to stay awake to assure myself of Rolf's safe return but drowsiness overcame my will power. It was Patch's growl which woke me. I expected to hear Rolf moving in the next room, instead I heard a key turning in the lock.

Instantly I was out of bed, tugging at the handle.

'Open this door,' I shouted, banging on it. 'Open it I say. How dare you lock me in. Open it whoever you are.'

The only answer was Patch's bark as he rubbed against my leg.

I was furious for allowing myself to be locked in again and puzzled as to who had the audacity to treat Rolf's guests in this presumptuous manner. I wondered what was happening in Marsh House after the servants had retired and if Rolf knew the secret or if he too was unknowingly locked in his room. It would explain his lack of knowledge concerning the nocturnal visitors.

My thoughts turned to the first Mrs. Cheval. Rolf had accused her of being fanciful. Had she too been locked in her room; heard mysterious carriages arrive and depart? Yet that was five years ago. Surely the same mystery could not exist for so long.

I propped myself into a sitting position with the pillows, determined to stay awake until my jailer returned. Then I had a better idea. The most satisfactory way to solve the puzzle was to be locked out, instead of in. I would say nothing of tonight's locked door, but tomorrow I would hide in the corridor. That way I would discover not only the person's identity but, with luck, also the reason for his or her behaviour.

8

When Rosie came into the room the next morning I asked if Rolf had returned.

'Yes, he brought the captains back with him.'

'What time was that?'

'I don't rightly know. It was after I went to bed.'

I stopped brushing my hair and, through the mirror, I watched her tidying away my night clothes.

'You must know. Yesterday you said that if visitors arrived during the night the maids were woken to attend them.'

'Oh, bless you, we don't look on the captains as guests, not like carriage folk. A room's always kept ready for them. They just come home with the master and go straight to bed. They don't bother us in the slightest.'

'Does this arrangement apply to all Mr. Cheval's captains?'

'No. Just Captains Easy and Lloyd. He treats them more like friends.'

I thought them strange friends for a man of his station, but it was not for me to comment on his choice of companions.

When I entered the breakfast room the three men were finishing their meal. Rolf saw me look questioningly at Captain Easy whose right arm was bound against his body.

'Captain Easy had an accident last night,' he explained,

as they reseated themselves after greeting me. 'His stallion stumbled into a deep rut and they both took a tumble.'

'I'm indeed sorry to hear it,' I said, smiling at Captain Easy. 'I trust no bones are broken.'

'Just a bad strain,' the Captain replied.

'In that case, I know just the potion for taking away the pain.'

'It's unnecessary for you to concern yourself, my dear,' Rolf replied. 'The Captain's already received all the medical treatment he requires.'

'But I'm positive that if Captain Easy'll permit me to massage his shoulder I can quickly bring him comfort. Old Daniel used to say I was an excellent hand at massaging away folks' pains. Do allow me to try.'

'You must remember you're not at the farm now, my dear. Here we have physicians to deal with such matters. They know a great deal more of the subject than you. They at least are taught to heal the sick.'

I blushed at the reprimand and an awkward silence befell us. Captain Easy glanced warily at Rolf, then said:

'I'm deeply obliged for your offer, ma'am, but it's not too painful. Rest is all I need.'

I was grateful for his attempt to ease the atmosphere, though I could tell from his face that the injury was worse than he pretended. The remainder of the conversation was strained and I was glad when the gentlemen departed.

In contrast to the previous day, the sun was shining and the weather so mild that one of the windows was standing open.

'I think I'll walk Patch in the grounds this morning,' I said, finishing my drinking chocolate.

'Not alone, madam?' Mason queried.

I smiled. 'If it'll make you happier, Rosie may come too.'

'Thank you, madam.'

It was delightful in the park, with the birds singing and the sun warm on our faces. The thawing snow had made the grass soggy, but we were wearing our boots and so were not hampered. Often in the distance we saw a pheasant or rabbit enjoying the springlike warmth. Patch chased everything which moved, while Rosie gave a résumé of the families living in the estate cottages.

'Is that where Mrs. Cheval died?' I asked, indicating a copse near the boundary wall. 'You say there's a cottage there?'

'Yes, but we'd be unwise to visit it now. The ground under the trees is too marshy. Besides, we've no leash for Patch. He could easily get lost in there.'

As always, I was aware of Rosie's strong sense of responsibility. Had she accompanied us yesterday the accident would not have occurred and old Daniel's brooch would not be at the bottom of the dyke. It was easy to understand why the first Mrs. Cheval had been so attached to her.

I contemplated mentioning my plans for trapping my jailor. It would be comforting to have an ally. Then I decided against it for Rosie might let the fact slip to the guilty person and then the mystery would never be solved. Only by keeping the scheme to myself could I be sure of its success.

Two enjoyable hours passed before we returned to the house.

'I'll take Patch to the kitchen and wash the mud from his paws,' Rosie said, as Mason met us in the vestibule.

'There's a gentleman waiting in the breakfast room, madam.'

'Not Lieutenant Stubbs again?' I said.

'A Mr. Layton. I told him you were not at home, but he insisted upon waiting. Do you wish to see him, madam?'

My pulse quickened. 'Yes, of course. Tell him I'll be down directly I've removed my bonnet.'

I climbed the stairs light of heart. It was foolish to be so excited, but I hummed merrily as I dabbed some rose water behind my ears and tidied my hair. Then I stepped back to check my appearance. My drab dress looked highly out of place in the splendid room but, as yet, I had nothing better to wear. I pinched some colour into my cheeks and wished Mrs. Harris had concentrated on making a day dress for me.

Downstairs Mason was waiting by the breakfast room door.

'You may announce me now,' I said, 'and then bring us a jug of hot chocolate.'

Mr. Layton turned from the window as I entered and I noticed how golden his hair looked in the sunlight.

'I trust you've completely recovered from your ordeal,' he said.

'Indeed yes, thanks to you. Won't you be seated?'

Mr. Layton flicked aside his coat tails and sat opposite me. 'I was afraid you'd catch a chill.'

'No. I'm quite well, thank you.'

My voice sounded too formal. Yesterday in the cottage everything had been natural and easy, as though we were friends of long standing. Now the harmony was missing. I was conscious of being the hostess; of needing to say the right thing.

The conversation died and I sought for another topic. My. Layton stood up and put his hand into the tail pocket of his coat.

'Forgive me calling in this unpardonable fashion, but the truth is, I wanted to return this.'

Nestling against his broad palm, was my pansy brooch. In my excitement I jumped up and crossed to him.

'Where'd you find it? I thought it had fallen into the dyke.'

'Beneath your chair. It probably fell when you took your coat off.'

'I'm so pleased to have it back. It was given to me by a dear friend. I value it for the memories it holds.'

At that moment Mason entered carrying a tray and I became embarrassingly aware of how close to Mr. Layton I was standing. I moved to a side table.

'Please put the chocolate here. I'll pour it myself.'

'As you wish, madam.'

He placed the tray before me and then hovered near the door, as though expecting me to request him to stay.

'Thank you, Mason. That will be all.'

He bowed and withdrew reluctantly.

'I'm sorry Mr. Cheval's not at home,' I said. 'I'm sure he'd have wished to make your acquaintance.'

'The disappointment is mine and I must bear full responsibility for calling uninvited.'

After a few more polite observations regarding the weather, he replaced his cup on its saucer and stood up.

'If you'll forgive me, I must take my leave now.'

His voice was as formal as his handshake. Here was a man I no longer knew. A return to the dour stranger who had started the journey from Wisbech with me. It was like losing a dear friend. Was this the effect Marsh House always had on people? I recalled my difficulties in talking freely with Rolf. I had thought that to be because we were not sufficiently well acquainted. Now the same impediment had occurred with Mr. Layton.

'I'll tell Mr. Cheval of your visit. Perhaps we can arrange for you to dine with us one evening.'

'That would be delightful.'

The reply was polite but lacking in any real feeling. Mason entered the moment I rang the bell.

'Mr. Layton's leaving,' I said.

I watched them go from the room, then I walked to the window. I saw Mr. Layton unfasten his horse from the hitching post and John assist him to mount. As he rode away I brushed aside the tears forming in my eyes. It was stupid to feel so downhearted. He was nothing to me; just an acquaintance.

I wandered up to my boudoir and seated myself by the fire with a book, but it was friendless there, for Patch had not yet been brought up from the kitchen.

The sound of approaching horses drew me to the window. Rolf and Captain Lloyd were returning and I envied them the business commitments which occupied their time.

For a while I watched the birds fluttering amongst the portico ivy, then I returned to my book. Presently Rosie entered looking flustered.

'Mr. Cheval wishes to see you in the library.'

'Has something happened to distress you? It's not Patch?'

'Oh, no. He's safe enough in the kitchen with everyone

making a fuss of him, but I think you'd best go down right away. The master's right put out about something.'

As I went downstairs I wondered what had happened to displease Rolf. Mason opened the library door for me and I saw Rolf seated at the mahogany desk which filled one corner of the room. His quill continued scratching across the parchment until he had finished the letter. He sanded and sealed it before looking at me with eyes cold as duelling swords.

'I presume you have an adequate explanation.'

Though I was both puzzled and frightened by his attitude, my voice remained firm.

'Explanation for what?'

'Your behaviour. What else? Don't you realize that the Cheval name must be above reproach? I won't have it degraded by anyone—most of all by you.'

'If you're referring to the incident on the beach, it was time those bullies were taught a lesson.'

'I'm not talking of that, although it was bad enough. I'm referring to your disgraceful behaviour with the Layton blackguard.'

I thought quickly. He was unlikely to be referring to yesterday for, to the best of my knowledge, the fog prevented anyone from seeing us enter or leave the cottage. Yet, facing Rolf, I realized the extent of my folly in hushing up the incident. A sensible person would have allowed Mr. Layton to ride for assistance and faced the possible humbling of her pride. If Rolf heard of it now it would be difficult to convince him of my innocence. Also, if Mason had reported Mr. Layton's call this morning it would be difficult to give Rolf an adequate reason for it. Yet, I must remain as near the truth as possible.

'I'm waiting for an explanation.'

'He . . . he came here to return a brooch which he thought belonged to me. He . . . saw me wearing it in the coach.'

Rolf's face became distorted with anger and in that instant I realized I must never become afraid of him, for once he learned of my fear, his mastery over me would be absolute.

'Are you telling me he had the audacity to come here—here to my house—I'll have him flayed before he's hanged.'

'Were you not talking of his visit?'

'No, madam, I was not. This is the first I've heard of the outrage.'

'What is so outrageous in a friend calling upon me?'

'Friend! Is that what you're pleased to call him? Lover is a better word. No-one will make a cuckold of me. No-one, hear you?'

Though my limbs were quaking I faced him bravely.

'I can hardly fail to. You're shouting so loud I should think the entire staff have heard you.'

He strode round the desk and grasped my wrist. 'I'll not accept insolence from any woman.'

The pain was intense but I refused to cry out. I had never yet allowed anyone to intimidate me, not even my step-mother, and I certainly had no intention of permitting Rolf to do so.

'Then I suggest you ask for an explanation with the manners of a gentleman.'

Instantly I regretted the hasty words for he twisted my arm until I thought the bones must surely snap.

'I'm a guest in this house and not yet your wife,' I said, wincing with pain. 'Nor am I ever likely to be—if this is a sample of your manners towards a lady.'

He gave my arm another twist, then released me so abruptly I stumbled against a chair and fell onto it. Instead of apologizing, he returned to his desk and sat down.

'There can be no excuse for what you did. The facts speak for themselves. You were enclosed in the cottage with him for over three hours. There can be only one reason for that.'

He spoke bitterly, as one wise to the world's sins and I felt a twinge of sympathy for him. If I was spied upon at the cottage, and particularly if the facts were exaggerated, the evidence against me must appear overwhelming.

'It's not as you think,' I said, and explained about the accident and rescue, adding: 'I realize I should have told you before now, but you weren't here last night and I could hardly mention it before your friends this morning.'

For a long time he sat staring at me. I began to feel as a mouse must feel before the cat pounces. The fire had gone from his eyes. They were icy cold now and calculatingly watchful.

'You do believe me?'

'I have your word. Is that not sufficient?'

His anger had been genuine; understandable and it contrasted ominously with this quietness. What manner of man could control his emotions so completely? There was an elusive quality about him which was disturbing. His fury, though excessive, was a natural reaction. Any man worthy of the name, who thought his fiancée was another man's mistress, was entitled to anger. But there was nothing natural in this unemotional acceptance.

'I'm sorry you had cause to think ill of me. I'll not keep secrets from you in future.'

'Indeed you won't. The Cheval name must be above gossip. In future you'll not leave this house without a chaperone.'

'But you have my word. I'll even promise never to speak to Mr. Layton again if that's your wish.'

'You have my orders. You'll go out with a chaperone or not at all. The servants'll be given instructions to that effect. As for this Layton fellow. I'll see he's suitably rewarded for saving your life. I'll also make it clear that his presence in this house is unwelcome and that any attempt to contact you again will not be tolerated. Now, if you'll excuse me, there are business matters needing my attention.'

Before I could argue he strode from the room, leaving the door swinging open behind him.

9

My emotions were in a turmoil. The knowledge that I had only myself to blame, added to my chagrin. Even so, Rolf's manner towards me was infamous and the thought of marrying someone so capable of inflicting pain was frightening. I wondered if Grandpa was aware of his sadistic tendency. As Rolf's wife I would be completely at his mercy, even Grandpa would be powerless to protect me.

I was troubled also by his decision to hasten the wedding. The reason he gave was not entirely satisfactory for, providing there were no fresh outbreaks of smallpox, I would be returning to the Hall shortly. It occurred to me that Rolf might have a reason for his haste of which I was unaware, for even in his anger at my suspected infidelity, he had not once threatened to cancel the marriage contract. The more I considered the matter, the more uneasy I became. I wished that old Daniel was nearer so that I might profit from his wisdom.

Rosie was waiting in my boudoir.

'Are you all right, Miss Debnam?' she asked anxiously.

Her question, coming immediately upon my own disturbing thoughts, caught me as being curious.

'Is there any reason why I shouldn't be?'

'No . . . no, of course not.'

'From your manner, I judge you to be thinking the opposite, so, if you please, I'll have the truth. Secrets are too plentiful in this house.'

'It's just that when Mrs. Elaine returned after being summoned like that, she was usually crying.'

'Was she indeed,' I said, realizing that my predecessor had made the mistake of allowing Rolf to intimidate her. 'I've no reason whatever to cry. Mr. Cheval merely

84

heard of my lateness in returning yesterday and wanted an account of the matter. Please order the carriage for me. I wish to visit my grandfather and I'll require you to accompany me.'

Rosie bobbed a curtsey, her face smiling once more.

'And bring Patch with you,' I called after her.

As we were descending the stairs, we met Rolf.

'I'm going to visit my grandfather,' I said, 'As both Rosie and the coachman'll be with me, I'll be quite adequately chaperoned.'

'Is that wise?' he asked. 'He sent you here to stop you from catching the smallpox. A visit'll not please him.'

'If he's afraid for me to enter the Hall, I shall ask him to walk in the park with me, or do you intend to forbid me to see him too?'

He had the grace to flush. 'If my manner towards you was presumptuous, it was not without good cause. However, I must apologize for any discomfort I caused you.'

Puzzled by his contrite manner, I glanced at him. His smile appeared quite genuine.

'It was partly my fault for not telling you the facts before you heard a garbled version,' I said.

He dismissed the subject by kissing my forehead. 'Enjoy your outing, my dear, but be sure you return before nightfall. It's too dangerous for you to be out after dark.'

The roads were soggy with slush and the ruts deep, but the sun was shining and Rosie lowered the carriage window so that the breeze might blow on our cheeks. She pointed out the places of interest. The white-washed dame school which Grandpa had founded; the better of the two bonnet shops; the wooden memorial to sailors lost at sea and the double fronted cottage where Mrs. Harris was making my new clothes. Beside the greensward we saw the barracks and the tall gun tower, built in panic during the days when Boney's invasion was imminent, but now standing neglected.

A glistening white cap tipped each wave as the ships glided like stately matrons towards their destinations.

One of the nearest bore Grandpa's flag, the others were too distant for me to distinguish their ensign without the aid of a spy-glass. The carriage turned inland between the rows of stunted osiers and all too soon we reached the Hall.

Unlike Marsh House, where a lackey came running down the steps immediately a carriage was sighted, no-one came out to greet us. As on my previous visit, when the maid eventually answered the jangling bell, she peered through the merest crack. This time, however, the chain was immediately removed.

'I'll tell Mrs. Gawthrop you be here.'

'It's Mr. Hawkins I wish to see,' I called, but she had already scurried away. A moment later Mrs. Gawthrop greeted me.

'I'm sorry you've been troubled,' I said. 'It's really my grandfather I wish to see.'

'Then I'm afraid your journey be wasted. He's away on business. Went yesterday and is not expected back for another two days.'

The news was disappointing. I had been counting on receiving his advice, not only about Rolf's behaviour, but also concerning the other happenings at Marsh House. Now there was no-one with whom I could discuss my problems.

Feeling obliged to give a reason for my visit, I said: 'I was hoping to learn when I might return here to live.'

'It's difficult to say. No-one else has caught the smallpox, so we're hoping it was halted in time. Mr. Hawkins reckons that after fourteen days we can consider ourselves safe.'

'What of the maid? Is she still here?'

'She died the day afore yesterday, poor soul. We buried her at once. We didn't want to take no chances.'

I left the house saddened by the knowledge of the girl's death. Alongside such news my own worries were quite trivial.

Rosie was standing beside the carriage talking to George, and Patch was sniffing his way across the lawn. Seeing him free to roam, reminded me of yesterday's near tragedy.

'Here, Patch,' I called.

Upon hearing my voice he came racing towards me, his tail wagging. I hugged him tightly before placing him in the carriage.

'On the way home we'll stop at Marshsea to buy him a collar and leash,' I said. 'Do you know of a good saddler?'

'Yes, next to Mrs. Long's teashop.'

Rosie was so obviously enjoying the outing I impulsively said: 'Then we'll make it a real excursion and visit the teashop too.'

'Do you mean it? I've never been to one before.'

I laughed. 'Truth to tell, neither have I.'

As the afternoon progressed it was easy to understand why my predecessor had been so fond of Rosie. The girl was a pleasing companion, without once forgetting her position was that of maid.

The teashop was quite dark inside, for little light penetrated the bow windows. The tea was exquisitely served by Mrs. Long, who looked as fragile as her china. Rosie and I laughed conspiratorially across the check table cloth and, for a while, I quite forgot the happenings at Marsh House.

Several customers came in to buy Mrs. Long's cakes, including a scarlet clad soldier with his befeathered girl, but no-one else stayed for tea. I thought I saw Mr. Layton pause to glance at the cakes displayed in the window and my heart quickened as I wondered what to do if he came inside, but he walked on and so the need for decision was averted. Later we noticed Lieutenant Stubbs strolling past with another officer.

'It seems that all Marshsea is taking the air this afternoon,' I said.

'It's the sun as brings them out,' Rosie replied, eating another piece of marchpane.

All too soon it was time for us to leave.

'The master'll not wish us to be out too late,' she said, 'not with so many soldiers and their followers about. Why, it's barely safe for a gentleman to be abroad after dark.'

As we stepped onto the cobble street we saw that

George had fallen asleep with the reins still in his hands. Rosie winked at me.

'Wake up, George,' she called. 'The master's waiting.'

'Oh . . . what . . .' To our merriment he awoke with such a start, he all but set the horses in motion. 'Oh, I beg your pardon, Miss Debnam. I didn't mean to fall asleep.'

He jumped from the box to open the carriage door. As I was placing Patch inside I noticed a letter lying on the seat.

'Who placed this in the carriage?' I asked.

'Blessed if I know, ma'am. I saw nobody do it.'

'It wasn't there when we got out,' Rosie said. 'Do you think someone tossed it through the window? We did leave it open.'

The seal was plain wax, but unlike the letter delivered yesterday, this one bore no recipient's name.

'I suppose it's meant for me,' I said, breaking the seal.

'Ought you to read it?'

From her look of concern, I realized that Rosie knew of Rolf's demand to inspect my future correspondence.

'I'm intrigued to know what it says.'

As before the message was cryptic.

'MRS. CHEVAL WAS INSIDE THE COTTAGE.'

'What is it? Why do you frown?'

'The oddest statement I've ever read.' I handed the note to her. 'Have you ever met the like? Why should anyone think such information interests me? Do you think it refers to the accident? If so, why tell me? It's no concern of mine.'

George regarded us anxiously. 'Might I ask what it says, ma'am?'

Upon hearing the message he rubbed the whip handle against his chin.

'If you'll pardon me saying so, ma'am. I reckon as how that message is meant for the master, 'cause if she was in that there old cottage, then I don't see as how she could have been shot by accident.'

'That's faddle,' Rosie retorted. 'It's my belief the letter was written by a body who wants to cause trouble. It stands to reason that, if Mrs. Cheval had been in the cottage, everyone would have known about it at the time.'

'Perhaps she was carried outside before anyone else reached her,' George argued. 'I always thought there was something rum about it.'

Rosie ignored him. 'The best thing is to give it to me and I'll burn it on the kitchen fire.'

I was not sure what to do. The previous letter had definitely stated I would be endangering my life by marrying Rolf. Now someone, possibly the same person, was hinting that Elaine's death was not an accident. Was there any truth in the allegation, or was it merely a malicious attempt to cause trouble? As Mr. Layton said, rich men have many enemies.

'I'll not do anything with it for the time being,' I said. 'It'd be doltish to worry Mr. Cheval unnecessarily, but if I receive more such letters, I'll certainly give them to him.'

Rolf was seated with his captains when I entered the ante-room that evening. After greeting me he said:

'You'll doubtless be pleased to know that I've dispatched a letter to Mr. Layton, thanking him for saving your life.'

'I appreciate that,' I said, realizing this was his way of asking me to forget the morning's contretemps. 'It was horrid not being able to thank him adequately.'

'I've also sent him a keg of brandy. Not much of a reward for so valuable a life, I grant you, but something a stranger might have difficulty in obtaining.'

'You mean it was contraband?'

He smiled. 'You really shouldn't look so disapproving.'

'But aren't you helping those beastly Frenchmen by accepting smuggled brandy?'

'I'm helping our townsfolk a great deal more. There's not many hereabouts who haven't a hand in the game.'

'Then you know who the smugglers are?'

The captains joined his laughter and I was dismayed that they should find my disapproval so amusing.

'Not exactly. A horse disappears in the night and is

back in its stable next day with a keg beside it. Like our late admiral, my eyes are not over anxious to see what doesn't concern them. Come, my dear, permit me to pour you a glass of Moselle, which I assure you I acquired by more traditional methods.'

As he spoke I was reminded of Mr. Layton's words, 'the fenmen ask no questions of their neighbour's business.' Now I knew why.

The meal passed pleasantly, although I realized that Captain Easy's arm was more painful than he admitted. Yet I was chary of renewing my offer to massage it.

When Mason placed the brandy on the table, I pleaded tiredness and bade them goodnight, for I knew their enjoyment would be freer without my company. Besides which, my thoughts were increasingly occupied by the forthcoming vigil and I wondered if my jailor was also connected with smuggling.

My door was usually locked about midnight, so I settled by the fire to read, but concentration was difficult. At eleven Rosie fetched Patch for his late night run. He went willingly and the room was lonely without him. He was a tiny fellow and already I had become accustomed to taking care not to step on him, for he had a tendency to stretch out on the floor wherever the fancy took him. A dangerous habit if it happened to be a spot not reached by candlelight.

When they returned I pretended to prepare for bed, but the moment the door closed behind Rosie, I threw back the covers and held a candle to the fire to relight it. I dressed quickly and added a thick woollen shawl, for I realized the corridor would be chilly.

Patch watched my activities with interest and whimpered when ordered back to bed. I hoped he would not bark when left alone.

I opened the door warily. The only candle was the one beside Rolf's room and the corridor was shadowy. Normally I am unafraid of darkness but tonight a thrill trickled along my spine as all the ghosts and ghouls of Daniel's stories crowded into my memory. It was easy to imagine some fiendish monster slinking into the pool of light supplied by the solitary candle. I had intended to secrete myself behind one of the velvet curtains, but I now realized it would be more advantageous to hide behind a massive Jacobean cupboard near my door. A person could pass quite close to it without being aware of my presence, yet I would have an excellent view of the corridor. I fetched a cushion from the boudoir and settled myself in the chosen niche.

At first I passèd the time by concentrating on all that had happened since my arrival, then I thought of old Daniel and the farm. Wondering if the lambs were all safely born; if the hens were laying well and if Daisy was giving an adequate supply now I was not there to milk her.

My limbs became cramped and I eased them to a more comfortable position. The corridor became colder. I pulled the shawl tighter about my shoulders and began counting backwards from a hundred. The landing clock had boomed twelve long ago. I wondered how much longer I dared stay, for if Rolf found me huddled there, he would certainly doubt my sanity. In fact, I was beginning to doubt it myself, wondering what had possessed me to hide here, instead of merely asking Mrs. Dobbs for the key as Rolf had suggested. The thought of snuggling in a warm bed was tempting. The jailor had not been this late before. Perhaps tonight he would not come. The clock boomed the half hour and I decided that if nothing happened by one I would return to bed.

To stop myself falling asleep I composed a poem about Patch. I was halfway through the second stanza when a cold draught swept along the corridor. It was gone instantly. I shivered and listened. There was no sound but the studious tock-tock of the grandfather clock at the head of the grand staircase.

Gradually I became aware of something moving. Nothing definite at first. Just the faintest impression that the far end of the corridor was becoming lighter. My heart raced, it was certainly much lighter now. I could distinguish the outline of the curtains covering the end window. The glow was coming from the servants' staircase and I was glad that my retreat was not cut off. Any moment now the person carrying the candle would turn the corner. Was it man or woman, young or old? My nerves were taut as I waited. The light was almost at the top now. Only another moment to wait.

My excitement became intense. I could hardly breathe. The candle came into view, then, whatever was holding it also became visible. I knew sheer terror. I had been so certain I would see a human being. Instead I was staring at a shapeless mass. I wanted to run but was too petrified to move. The candlelight magnified the grotesque shadow it cast on the wall. Was this what the first Mrs. Cheval had seen?

It stopped by my door. I saw a glint of metal as the key was inserted in the lock. It turned, was withdrawn and then hidden beneath a vase standing on a chest. My fear faded. Ghosts could not turn keys, that was the prerogative of the living. This was someone wearing a black cloak with the hood pulled well over the head so that the face was also concealed. I was undecided what to do. Accuse the figure or wait to see what happened next. I decided upon the latter, for only by following could I hope to learn more.

Expecting the apparition to return down the servants' staircase, I prepared to stand up. Instead it turned in my direction. For an instant I thought I had been seen, but it passed me so closely I could have touched the cloak, and I detected a slight trace of perfume. From the rustle of skirts I guessed it to be a woman.

She opened the door leading to the main house and stood listening for sounds from below. Then the door closed and she was gone.

Despite my cramped limbs I moved quickly. I had no intention of losing my quarry now. I opened the door cautiously. She was moving down the stairs like a great black shadow. I was glad the only light was from the sconces in the vestibule, for it meant I was standing in darkness. I moved stealthily to the banister. She was nearing the bottom step. Suddenly I realized the reason for the heavy cloak. She was going out into the night.

Now I was in a quandary. The temperature outside was below freezing and I had only a shawl for protection.

Then, to my astonishment, she ignored the front entrance and crossed instead to the breakfast room.

I waited till the door closed behind her, then I sped down the stairs. I would catch her in the act of doing whatever required so much secrecy. I reached the door and threw it open. The room was empty. A fact which did not surprise me, for I had already guessed she was probably making for the library beyond. So, without stopping to consider the consequences, I rushed to the inner door.

It is difficult to say who was the most startled. I by the scene before me, or the occupants by my sudden and spectacular entrance. Whatever I had expected to see it was certainly not Rolf and the captains lolling in chairs by the fire, each the worse for brandy. Rolf rose to his feet and clung to the back of his winged chair for support.

'Henney, my dear. Come in.' His words were slurred. 'Sorry there's no brandy left.'

'I didn't come here to drink. Where is she?'

Rolf collapsed back onto the chair. 'Where's who, m'dear?'

It was obvious that her reason for coming here had little to do with Rolf. He was in no state to entertain a guest.

'The hooded figure who came in here.'

'The hooded figure . . .' he began laughing.

Captain Easy, who was slightly less drunk, looked puzzled. 'No-one's been here since Mason went to bed.'

'But I saw her. At least I saw her enter the ante-room and she's not there now. She must have come in here.'

'I assure you she didn't. Look for yourself. There's nowhere to hide, unless it's behind the curtains and no-one's there.' He lurched towards them, and with his uninjured arm, held back each in turn.

Rolf stopped laughing and turned to Captain Lloyd. 'Isn't it the curse of my luck. I've already had one damned ghost seeing woman, now I'm to be saddled with another. Here's my advice, gentlemen. Never take a wife if you respect your sanity.'

93

'She was not a ghost,' I retorted. 'Whoever came in here was as much alive as any of us.'

Captain Easy shook his head. 'I'm sorry, ma'am, but you can't have it both ways. Either it was a ghost or you mistook the door she entered. You may have my word that not a living soul but yourself has come in here for the last two hours . . . unless, yes, that's possible . . . there are curtains in the ante-room too, you know.'

Without a word I returned to where the table was laid for breakfast and whisked back the curtains, but I knew it was a forlorn hope. My quarry had ample time to slip from the room while I was talking in the library. I was annoyed with myself for not having looked behind these curtains on my way through, but I had been so sure that she was heading for the library. It had not occurred to me that she knew I was following her and had entered this room to trick me.

Now, not only did my jailor know of my interest in her nocturnal activities, but I had also made a fool of myself before the captains and given Rolf cause to think I was as fanciful as Elaine. I was even more angry with myself later that night when it occurred to me that, by showing Rolf the key, I could have proved the woman existed.

Yet, at least I had ascertained one thing. Neither Rolf nor his captains were connected with the mystery.

10

'Miss Debnam, are you there? Are you all right?'

My deep slumber was shattered by a thumping noise and for a moment I was confused. I thought it still night until I pulled back the nearest bed curtain and saw the sun's golden light.

"Who is it?' I called, still befuddled by sleep.

'Me, Rosie. I can't open the door. Are you all right?'

'Yes, of course. Just a moment, I'll open it for you.'

I took the key from beneath my pillow and, as I opened the door, I was shocked by Rosie's agitation.

'Why the alarm?'

Rosie made an effort to control herself. 'It was the door being locked. I pictured all kinds of horrid possibilities. I didn't know you had a key.'

As I covered my nightshift with the cambric peignoir, I told her about my vigil and how I followed the woman downstairs.

'Oh, Miss; you shouldn't do such things, not without me to protect you. Fancy you daring to follow the ghost like that.'

'It was no ghost, I assure you.'

Rosie's agitation increased and she spoke quickly:

'It *was* the ghost, for I've seen her too. Dressed just as you said. She comes down the servants' stairs, along this passage and down the grand stairway to the vestibule, where she melts into the shadows.'

Rosie's admission surprised me, as did her reluctance to meet my eyes.

'The other day you said you hadn't seen her.'

She turned from me and busied herself clearing the ash from yesterday's fire and replacing it with kindling.

'I know, and I'm sorry for deceiving you. I was frightened you might want to go searching for her like Miss Elaine did. There's a terrible legend that those who follow the ghost, follow it into eternity.'

I watched her relighting the fire. Her movements were unusually clumsy. Until this moment I had considered her to be particularly level headed. The last person to be given to fanciful superstitions.

'You cannot seriously expect me to believe that she followed the ghost out to the wood and was shot. The accident happened in full daylight.'

With a suddenness which caught me completely unawares, she stood and gripped my arm.

'You must believe me. You must promise never to go searching for that ghost again.'

'You're hurting me.'

Though she relaxed her grip, there was no mistaking the tenseness of her emotions.

'Please, Miss Debnam, for my sake, meddle not with things you don't understand. Mrs. Elaine followed that ghost and two days later she died. It's not just a legend. It really happens, so for mercy's sake promise you'll never go following it again. If you like, I'll sleep in here on a truckle bed. I'll gladly make do, if it'll keep you safe.'

Though I could not believe in such nonsense, I was much affected by Rosie's conviction.

'Don't distress yourself,' I said, 'now I have the key and know about the legend, I'll lock my door and not go stalking ghosts at the witching hour.'

'You promise? You give me your solemn word?'

'I give you my most solemn promise that I'll not leave this room at night in search of a ghost. Will that suffice?'

'Oh, yes, Miss. I'll rest much easier now.'

I smiled: there was no sense in agitating her unnecessarily. The promise was easy enough to give. I had pledged never to follow a ghost, but it was no ghost I intended to follow. It was a living, breathing woman, and nothing had been said about following such a person. It would be interesting to see what happened tonight. Was the woman's nocturnal prowl so important she would chance another walk? One thing was certain. The next time I followed her, I would not be so easily hoodwinked.

That morning I was spared the embarrassment of meeting Rolf and the captains, for they were late rising. A fact which scarcely surprised me, considering their condition during the night. I ate a leisurely breakfast, then told Rosie my intention to walk Patch in the park.

'Shall I come with you?' she asked.

'No, I'd rather you visited Mrs. Harris and collected the gown she promised to finish today. If it's not ready, then wait until it is. I'm ashamed of my old dress. I cannot conceive what Mr. Cheval's friends must think of me.'

Patch at first objected to wearing a collar, but the excitement of going out soon won his attention.

For once Mason was not in the vestibule but, even so, my departure was noted. As I turned to take a stick from Patch, I saw Briggs following me, and I realized the servants had been told not to allow me out alone. For a moment I was furious and tempted to order Briggs to return. Then I thought he was merely carrying out Rolf's orders and probably disliked them as much as I. Providing he did not intrude upon my enjoyment of the spring-like morning, there was little to be gained by creating trouble.

The grass was now clear of snow and in several places the coltsfoot added vivid patches of yellow. Out here in the bright park, thoughts of locked doors and mysterious women creeping through corridors gained a dream-like quality. The house, standing majestically amid the greenery, looked too serene to hide any frightening secrets.

In the distance a cheeky hare was practising its mating dance. Patch saw it and was off like an arrow. As I pushed his leash into my pocket my hand touched yesterday's note.

I was intrigued by the singular message. What possible interest could the exact whereabouts of Mrs. Cheval's death be to anyone now? I looked at the copse. It was odd that no-one had witnessed the accident. As I drew nearer I called Patch to heel and fastened the leash to his collar, for I had no wish to lose him amongst the dead bracken and fallen leaves. Though the branches were bare, they were so close together, the atmosphere was dark and forbidding. At first there was no path to guide me over the squelching ground then, quite suddenly, I came upon one wide enough to admit a cart. I followed it expecting to arrive at the cottage. Instead I emerged on the far side. From the occasional sound of snapping twigs I knew that Briggs was still following me. I turned and called.

'Briggs, where are you?'

There was a pause, then his answering voice.

'Here, madam. Can I help you?'

He emerged not ten yards from where I was standing.

'I'm told there's a cottage in the wood. Can you take me to it?'

'Certainly, madam, though it's in a sorry state of repair. No-one visits it since the mistress died. It's this way.'

He indicated back along the path.

'Were you at the fatal shoot?'

'No, madam. Only the senior servants accompanied the master.'

Now Briggs was away from Mason's supervision he lost his reticence and became willing to talk.

'That's a pity. I was hoping you might be able to show me exactly where she died.'

'I can do that. I heard the others talking about it.' He stopped walking and pointed to a narrow path leading off to our right. 'The cottage is along there.'

The narrow track was littered with wet bracken, so I lifted Patch into one arm and held my skirts close about my legs with my free hand. About a hundred yards from the main path we rounded a bend and there was the cottage.

It was certainly dilapidated. A bird's nest was lodged between the broken shutter and the window. The thatched roof sagged and moss clouded the cobbled walls.

'It's a strange place to build a cottage. Who lived here?'

'I don't rightly know. There are them as says it was built to hide the Cavaliers waiting to cross the sea.'

I remembered Lieutenant Stubbs' warning that French prisoners were known to be hiding in the district. Was history repeating itself? It would make an ideal sanctuary. I looked at Briggs. He was probably in his mid-twenties and several inches taller than I. His shoulders were broad enough to tackle any foe. I was glad of his protective company for, if there were any prisoners hiding in the cottage, at least I would not be facing them alone.

I was determined not to let Briggs see my apprehension as I lifted the latch. The door opened easily, almost as though it had been recently oiled. Cautiously I pushed it wider, half expecting to hear a startled oath from within, but all was quiet.

The interior consisted of one large room. On the far side was a cupboard bed, with one door sagging open. From it protruded a gnawed palliasse, its straw spilling onto the earth floor. On either side of the spider festooned fireplace was a tall cupboard. The nearest contained a conglomeration of tin mugs and plates, so blackened with dust it was impossible to tell their original colour, though, strangely enough, a candle and its holder looked comparatively clean. The other cupboard was completely empty; not even a shelf furnished it. The room reeked of decay and I was glad to step back into the fresh air.

'Pity it's so neglected. It'd make a good home for some poor soul,' I said.

'None of the folk hereabouts would have it. They say that on moonlight nights the mistress still walks here.'

'Come now. I cannot believe such nonsense.'

'You ask Will Blakely, the gamekeeper. He's seen her with his own eyes. You'll not get him near the place after nightfall, and there's none I knows of tougher than him.'

'Did he see her face?'

'Not him. He wouldn't come that near, but it had to be her. No-one else had reason to haunt this old cottage.'

'It was probably a poacher dressed up to frighten him off. If the gamekeeper's too frightened to come near these woods, then obviously, the poachers can do as they please.'

'There bain't no cause to poach here 'cause, after Mrs. Cheval died, the master gave orders that anyone could catch the rabbits. He didn't mind who came as long as they kept down the vermin.'

'And yet no-one comes?'

'Not even them as are starving. They say it's an evil place.'

'You're here now.'

'So are you, begging your pardon, ma'am. My orders are wherever you goes, I got to go.'

'Even if it means facing a ghost?'

'I'd sooner face a ghost than the master's wrath if anything happened to 'e. 'Side's it be daylight now, and I reckon as how the mistress were that gentle in life she wouldn't harm me now.'

'Where exactly did she die?'

'Just here by this great tree.' He walked some five yards away to where an oak stood alien beside the beech trees. 'I reckon as how she were leaning against the trunk when it happened. You see, if she were just here and moved her head sharpish like, with it being so dark in the wood in summer, someone might have seen a patch of sunlight on her face and mistook it for the white belly of a squirrel. Shadows can play funny tricks in a wood.'

'That doesn't explain why she was shot with a pistol, and not a fowling piece.'

'Aye, that's the rub. There's no-one that can fathom that, for not one of the gentlemen was carrying a pistol.'

'You're sure she was shot by this tree and not in the cottage. She could have staggered out afterwards.'

'No, ma'am. She were sitting here right enough. You ask anyone.'

My fingers touched the note. Why did the writer insist she died in the cottage? What difference did it make?

'Who was the first to find her?'

'Mr. Mason. It upset him so much he refuses to discuss it, though the other servants still talk about it.'

'Do you think it possible he killed her—accidentally, I mean?'

'No, ma'am, he and the other servants were the carriers and beaters, they didn't have no guns. It were a terrible thing; we couldn't believe it. She was such a good lady.'

'But a little fanciful, I believe?'

'She said she saw a ghost in Marsh House, but the master wouldn't have that there was one.'

'Now she's the ghost herself. Is that not a little strange?'

'Many old houses have two ghosts.'

'Do they indeed? Have you heard tell what happens to anyone who sees the Marsh House ghost?'

'They gets a fright, I reckon.'

'Is there no legend connected with it?'

'Not that I knows of.'

I thought of Rosie's agitation this morning and her conviction that the ghost was responsible for Mrs. Cheval's death, and wondered whether Briggs had really not heard of the legend, or if he was pretending ignorance.

As I returned to the house storm clouds were obscuring the sun. I was glad I had taken an early stroll for the best of the day was obviously over.

In answer to my query, Mason told me that Rosie had not yet returned and that Mr. Cheval and his guests were not expected home until nightfall.

When I returned to my room after luncheon, a steady drizzle was falling, blotting out the sea view and covering the landscape with a dismal haze. There would be little pleasure in walking or riding this afternoon. I poked the fire into a more cheerful blaze and sat near it, tickling Patch's head as he scrambled into the chair beside me.

My thoughts were still full of the mystery woman. To the best of my knowledge, I was the only female guest, yet there had definitely been a woman's laugh the night the coach came.

Thinking I might find the answer in another part of the house, I tugged the bell pull. I might be only a visitor at the moment, but within a few weeks I would be the mistress. That surely gave me the right to be shown round.

When one of the maids answered the summons, I dispatched her to Mrs. Dobbs' room with a message that I wanted to see her.

The housekeeper arrived looking worried.

'Mary said you wanted me. I trust nothing's wrong?'

'It's such a vile afternoon I thought it might be an ideal opportunity for me to become better acquainted with my future home. Will you conduct me?'

'Certainly, Miss Debnam, if that be your wish.'

As she turned to lead the way towards the grand-stairway I stopped her.

'I'd rather go this way, if you don't mind,' I said, pointing to the servants' stairs.

They were too narrow for us to walk abreast, so I went first. At the top Mrs. Dobbs paused to regain her breath, then opened the nearest door.

'This floor of the west wing is composed mostly of the children's rooms. Mr. Rolf learned his lessons at that table, but he was a lonely mite.'

'Had he no playmates?'

'He had two brothers and three sisters, but they died in infancy. His parents were that frightened of losing him, they went to all lengths to keep him safe. Hence the iron bars across the windows. He was an adventurous lad and this room's three flights up. They were afraid he might climb out and fall.'

I crossed to the window and looked down. The ground was a good forty feet below. 'They were wise. Anyone falling from this height would surely be killed.'

'He hated being treated like an invalid. Sometimes he would hide and, try as we might, we couldn't find him. The whole household would be put into a turmoil, every room searched; every nook and cranny, but we never found him until he wanted to be found. Even today I still don't know where he hid. Many a time I've asked him, but he just laughs and says we should have searched more thoroughly. It was one of those escapades which killed his poor mother.'

'I didn't know that.'

Mrs. Dobbs seated herself on the rocking chair and set it in slow motion, as though rocking herself back into the past.

'It happened when his father was in France. A soggy day, just like this. Mr. Rolf was in a paddy because his mama had forbidden him to go riding. He had a terrible temper in those days. When Mr. Long, he was the butler at the time, stopped him going out of the front door, he picked up a priceless vase and smashed it beyond repair. That was the only time I saw Mistress Isobel really angry. She ordered Mr. Rolf to be whipped. His shouts and curses were dreadful to hear. Even so, Mistress Isobel stayed by until the punishment was over. Then she went to her room and locked herself in. When she came down to dinner that night Mr. Rolf was nowhere to be found. The servants searched all night and all the next day, but there was no trace of him. He had just vanished.'

'Run away?'

'No, he was here somewhere but we couldn't find him. The mistress was beside herself with worry. Nothing could pacify her. That afternoon she collapsed. She died before the physician could reach her. It's my belief she thought she had killed him and died of a broken heart, for nothing we could say would make her believe he was still alive.'

'When was he found?'

'That very night.' She stood up and led the way into the next room. 'The governess found him there, fast asleep in that very bed. Just as though he had been there all the time. Yet we searched every inch of this old house and could have sworn he was not in it.'

'Was he greatly upset by his mother's death?'

'It's difficult to say with Master Rolf. Because he didn't cry, there were them as said he didn't care, but to me, that's not true. I think that, though he was only twelve, he was too proud to show his real feelings. He kept them bottled up inside. Ah, poor soul, he needed all the courage the good Lord could give him that week, for two nights later fate dealt another cruel blow. There was a dreadful storm; the lightning was terrible to see. Many a good brig was lost that night, including the one bringing his father back from France. The winds blew it onto the Goodwin sands. There were no lifeboats worth the name in those days; nothing to save the poor souls from drowning. Master Rolf began that week as a naughty boy and ended it as a man. Aye, the poor master's known his share of trouble, so you must bear with him if he's a mite out of temper at times. He needs a sensible wife like yourself to teach him to laugh again.'

'Was he not happy with the first Mrs. Cheval?' I could not refrain from asking the question. I felt I had to know everything if I was to understand and help him.

As though to occupy her hands, Mrs. Dobbs straightened the patchwork quilt covering the unused bed.

'We thought so at first. Then she began to imagine things, saying she saw strangers in the house at night. He was angry; said she was talking nonsense. Once I heard him threaten to send her to an asylum if she continued to allow her imagination to play false. After that, she never mentioned them again, but I know she still believed she heard them.'

'Is it possible that she really did? It's a large house, wouldn't it be possible for someone to hide here without anyone knowing?'

'Not in those days, the house was usually full of guests.'

I crossed to the barred window and looked down at the rainswept garden, remembering the night I heard a carriage below. Rosie had sworn no-one arrived that night.

'Did she live in these parts before her marriage?'

'Bless you, no. She was a city lady, born and bred. If you ask me that was part of her trouble. She was not used to country ways. Parties and the playhouses were more to her liking. It was boredom that started her fancies.'

I felt sympathy for her, for I too sensed a strange loneliness about this great house though unlike her, I was used to spending a great deal of my time alone. Solitude had not previously bothered me, yet here it was all too easy to allow one's fancies to wander; to make mysteries where there were none. Suddenly I wanted to be free of this room where Rolf had slept unaware of his mother's death.

'Come, let's continue the tour. You say there are other bedrooms in this corridor?'

Mrs. Dobbs led the way into the ones once used by the nursery staff. Each had the musty odour of unused rooms and all the furniture was covered with dust sheets.

We stepped from the corridor into the main house and I opened the nearest door expecting to see another bedroom. Instead I was standing in a magnificent reception room, some thirty feet long by twenty wide. The blue ceiling was edged with white plaster flowers and from each corner a plump cherub leaned forward with a bunch of grapes clutched in chubby hands.

A crystal chandelier hung from the centre, and matching candle holders were fixed to the walls between the gilt mirrors which reflected the polished floor and striped sofas. My imagination filled the room with the gay people who had danced at Rolf's wedding celebrations, and I was disappointed there was no talk of a ball to celebrate mine. Yet it was understandable that Rolf might have no desire to be reminded of his first marriage and intended the arrangements for his second to be simple as possible.

As though reading my thoughts, Mrs. Dobbs said:

'Mayhap when you're mistress things'll be different. This room should be used to give pleasure to the living.'

I agreed with her. It was meant to be enjoyed, not shut off like an unwanted relic. Yet neither Grandpa nor Rolf had taken the slightest step to introduce me to the local society, and not one person had called to leave their card, though many must know of my presence at Marsh House. It was surprising that curiosity had not brought a few callers.

With smallpox at the Hall, Grandpa was not in the position to entertain, but Rolf at least could have introduced me to some of the local gentry. Still, I could scarcely expect him to be proud of me in my shabby clothes. Perhaps he was waiting until my new ones were ready before launching me.

Two of the rooms in the east wing were obviously being used by the captains, for fires burned in the grates. The furniture in the others was shrouded.

We paused at the servants' staircase, a replica of the one in the west wing.

'Above here are the attics where the lower servants sleep,' Mrs. Dobbs said. 'Two large dormitories and three smaller rooms for the men in this wing, and the same for the women in the west.'

'Is there nothing else up there?'

'Only the lumber rooms where the unwanted furniture is stored.'

'I would like to see them,' I said, for as yet the tour had revealed nothing to indicate that an unknown person might be living in the house.

The lumber rooms too revealed no clues and I was left with only two possibilities. Either the woman was a servant, or ghosts had the power to lock doors, and I refused to believe the latter.

When I returned to my room Patch jumped from his box and ran whimpering to the door. Realizing that it was several hours since his last run, I pulled on my coat and took him downstairs. The rain had ceased and, although it was not quite dark, the candles were already lit. It was the first time I had ventured out in the evening and I was impressed by the house's splendour as the large windows radiated a glowing welcome. As I walked along the carriageway for a more distant view, I noticed the candles in the tower were also alight, and thought of the brigs being guided home.

I noticed Briggs was walking discreetly behind me and hoped he would not catch a chill, for he was wearing no coat over his livery and the evening air was decidedly cold.

This was the second time I had left the house, as I thought unobserved, only to find myself being followed.

'Briggs,' I said. 'How is it that I've twice left the house without seeing anyone and each time you've followed me?'

'Mr. Mason told me to come, ma'am.'

'How, pray, did Mr. Mason know I was out?'

'I can't say, ma'am,' he replied, avoiding my eyes.

'Then tell me this. Are my movements deliberately spied upon?'

'I can't say, ma'am.'

His reticence answered the question, but at least no-one was interfering with my activities. I was free to do exactly as I pleased within the limits of decorum. It was amusing that Rolf should consider me so in need of protection.

I called Patch to heel and walked back towards the house. The little remaining daylight had gone now and the moon had not risen yet. The uncurtained windows looked gay with the candlelight shining through them.

I was surprised to see that the library was lit, for I had not realised Rolf was home. From where I stood only the top half of the room was visible. The centre chandelier was in darkness, but the wall candles were flaming, lighting up the great mirror over the mantle. I was about to move on when something in the reflection caught my eye. The mirror was hanging in such a position that the top jutted from the wall. Thus, although the window sill hid the furniture from my direct view, I could see it reflected in the looking glass.

I blinked and stared harder, wondering if my eyes were deceiving me, but no, it was still there in the bottom left hand corner. On the sofa a couple were locked in the tenderest embrace. As I watched they parted and the man lifted the woman's hand to his lips, his other hand caressing her black hair. I was too overcome to move. All I could do was stare at the lovers. She was dressed in the height of fashion and certainly put my clothes to shame. Even the indistinctness of the reflected image could not mar her beauty.

The man was Rolf.

It was Patch tugging at my skirt which broke the spell. Instinctively I bent down to lift him into my arms, but he was playful and it was several minutes before I had him secure. Then I became aware of Briggs hovering nearby.

'Who's the woman in the mirror?' I asked.

He glanced into the lighted room, then shuffled his feet uneasily.

'Well?' I demanded.

My eyes followed his to the reflection, and I knew why he was reluctant to reply.

Rolf was seated alone on the sofa reading a book.

11

Someone had warned her that I was outside. I tripped over my skirt in my haste to reach the vestibule while she was still there. Heavens knows what impression Briggs received as I raced up the portico steps with Patch struggling in my arms.

Mason, who was coming out of the breakfast room, looked startled by my abrupt entrance. 'Is something amiss, Madam?'

I glanced round. The log fire was bright in the far corner; nothing moved on the staircase or on the gallery above. It was impossible for anyone to reach the sanctuary of either wing so quickly, so she must still be in the library. Before Mason could object, I entered the breakfast room, crossed it quickly and opened the library door.

Rolf was alone, seated as I had last viewed him, with one arm resting along the sofa back and the other holding a book. It was a homely scene, with nothing to indicate he had not been alone all afternoon. The sudden draught caused the fire to splutter and he glanced up.

'Henrietta, my dear, you're exceedingly flushed. Are you feeling ill?'

Nonplussed I stared at him. There had not been time for the woman to escape, yet where was she?

Rolf stood up, looking incredibly handsome in his blue velvet jacket and white stock.

'Allow Mason to take your puppy to the kitchen, my dear, and sit by the fire with me. It's seldom we have the opportunity to talk alone. Mason,' he added, to the butler now hovering in the doorway, 'take Miss Debnam's coat and bring us both a glass of Madeira. Frown not,' he said, looking at me. 'It's a trifle early for drinking I grant, but you appear quite chilled. Only the foolish venture out on a day like this, my dear. There are ample servants to walk your dog. It's not in the least necessary for you to do it.'

I sat down, shuddering as I recalled the reflected scene. Thinking I was cold, Rolf poked the fire to a bigger blaze.

'You must take more care, my love. It will not do to be ill on our wedding day. It's only a sennight away.'

His blue-green eyes regarded me with such frank concern it was difficult to believe that a few minutes ago he had kissed another woman—or had he? Was it possible that I, like Elaine, was seeing things? Surely not. Yet Briggs had not seen her and her ability to disappear certainly needed explaining.

I realised that Rolf was apologising for being in his cups last night and I forced a smile.

'I should be the one to apologise for intruding upon you so late at night.'

He sat beside me and rested an arm along the sofa behind my shoulders. 'My recollections are a trifle blurred. I seem to remember you were expecting to find someone with us, but for the life of me, I cannot remember who it was.'

I hesitated. If I told him the truth he might think my imagination was following Elaine's example, yet he was entitled to an explanation. As I had previously spoken of the locked door, I decided to risk telling him of my vigil. When I finished, he asked:

'Where's the key now?'

'Here in my reticule.'

'Then keep it safe, my dear. Lock the door on the inside tonight and stop worrying. The servants are here to deal with such matters. I'll speak to Mason. If anyone is wandering the house at night, he'll discover the reason, you can rely on that. It's probably nothing more alarming than a servant keeping a lover's tryst.'

'Rosie suggested it was a ghost, which explains why it disappeared.'

He raised a quizzical eyebrow. 'Unfortunately young Rosie was too attached to my first wife. I suppose you've been told of the non-existent things she saw and heard.'

'Then you don't think it was a ghost?'

'My dear Henrietta. I cannot pretend to be an authority on such matters, but it seems distinctly unlikely that a ghost can lock doors.'

His words brought little comfort. If there were no ghosts, then whose reflection had I seen in the mirror, and where was she now?

I was delivered from the temptation of questioning Rolf by Mason's announcement of Rosie's return. To my delight she had brought not one, but two gowns.

A brown paisley with ruched sleeves for the mornings and one of rich blue velvet for evenings.

'That suits you wonderfully well,' Rosie said, standing back to admire the blue one. 'The high waist and unbroken skirt line is most becoming. The master'll be proud of you tonight.'

Rolf was indeed pleased by my appearance when I joined the gentlemen for dinner.

'You look charming, my dear. Perfectly charming.'

The admiration in his eyes was unmistakable and I was happy that he was pleased.

That night I waited again for the woman to appear but, by one thirty, I realized that she was not coming. Disappointed and cold, I undressed and climbed into bed. I wished I had a warming pan, for the linen sheets were icy against my legs. A door banged as Rolf came upstairs, then all was silent. I tossed restlessly on the feather bed, my thoughts constantly returning to the mirror reflection. Was it merely a trick of the candlelight which had made Rolf appear to be kissing someone? Certainly there was no time for a human to leave that room before I entered and, unlike last night, the curtains had not been closed.

Suddenly my drowsiness vanished. I sat up in bed, my mind fully alert. Last night the woman had entered the breakfast room and disappeared. Today's woman had also disappeared there.

I took the candle from the bedside table and lit it at the fire. The answer was so simple, I was annoyed for not thinking of it before. Briggs had spoken this morning

110

of the Cavaliers hiding in the cottage. If this house had been owned by Royalists then the chances were it had a secret hiding place and where more likely than the panelled breakfast room?

Excited by the possibility I pulled on my peignoir and added my coat for warmth, before quietly opening my door. All the house candles were extinguished and my own flickering light cast moving shadows over the walls. My hands trembled as I crept downstairs and across the vestibule. All round me the darkness was thick and deep. I needed to remind myself that ghosts did not exist, that they were only figments of Elaine's imagination.

I opened the breakfast room door and stood listening. In the grate of the massive marble fireplace a few embers gleamed red. My candlelight flickered over the breakfast table and silver cutlery. The tapestry curtains were closed, so I looked behind them to assure myself no-one was hiding there. Then I lit the sconce candles and was glad of their light which dispelled the gloomy shadows.

Starting from the doorway, I worked systematically, tapping each panel, listening for any indication of hollowness. When that failed, I turned my attention to the carved flowers and leaves, twisting and pressing each in the hope of releasing a hidden spring.

The room became colder and some candles burned out. Yet, the more I thought of it, the more convinced I was that a secret place existed. Apart from the woman's ability to disappear at will, it would also explain why Rolf was able to hide so successfully when a child. That conjecture was disquieting for, if the woman really existed and Rolf was in love with her, it was imperative that I knew the truth before I was irrevocably committed to him.

I opened the library door and stood looking at the book lined walls. It was unlikely that any of those weighty cases would swing aside. Besides, last night the captains had been in this room. It was doubtful if the woman would open the panel in their presence. It must be located in the breakfast room and yet, I had tried

111

all the likely places. I wished Mr. Layton were here to help me.

The landing clock chimed five, reminding me not to dally longer. The maid would soon be rising to light the fires and I had no wish for her to find me here. The wisest policy was to go to bed now, and get the maximum rest during the day, so I would be fresh to continue the search tomorrow night.

Several times during the following hours I was tempted to take Rosie into my confidence but was afraid of making a fool of myself.

That night the wait for Rolf to come to his room seemed endless. Several times I stepped onto the landing to listen for sounds of him coming upstairs. At last, frustrated by the wait and fearful of falling asleep, I placed a tinder box in my pocket and, taking an unlighted candle, crept downstairs to hide behind the breakfast room curtains until he left the library. That way I would gain the advantage of being able to start the search the moment he went upstairs.

I guessed from their laughter that he and the captains were drinking freely. I wondered if Rolf habitually drank too much or whether he was merely being a good host to his guests who were, after all, seafaring men and probably used to consuming quantities of brandy.

Though the clock boomed one-thirty, there was no sign of the revelry ending and I began to regret my foolishness in coming downstairs. It could easily be an hour or two before they eventually parted. Once I thought I heard a woman's laugh mingling with theirs and I chastised myself for allowing my imagination too much freedom.

Then I became aware of another noise. One I had certainly not imagined. I peeped between the curtains and saw the vestibule door open and the hooded woman enter. Hardly daring to breathe for fear of betraying myself, I watched her creep to the library door and stand with her ear against it. Apparently satisfied, she moved to the fireplace. I tried to will her to turn round so I could see her face, but her back remained towards me.

At first I thought she was warming herself, then I

watched fascinated as a slab of marble surround swung inward, revealing a cavity. She lit her candle from one in a sconce and turned to negotiate with her foot, what appeared to be a ladder leading downwards.

For an instant her face was towards me and I nearly betrayed myself so great was my astonishment. I am not sure who I expected it to be. A stranger perhaps, or, as Rolf had suggested, one of the kitchen servants. Instead I saw the one person I least expected. It was my own maid, Rosie.

I could scarcely believe my eyes. Yet, even as I watched her descend, pieces of the bewildering puzzle fell into place. This explained why none but the Cheval brides saw the ghost; why Rosie was frightened when I expressed my intention of discovering the truth; why Briggs had not heard of the legend.

Yet, why should Rosie invent the ghost and go walking in secret passages at night? I doubted if a lover's tryst would apply to her.

As she reached up to pull a closing lever, the hood slipped from her head. In that second I knew the answer. When Lieutenant Stubbs called the other evening to warn us about the French prisoners, he said:

'We know a black haired lady is assisting their escape.'

Rosie's hair, though not as dark as mine, could be mistaken for black in a poor light. Without a shadow of doubt, the traitor who was betraying her country by helping the enemy to escape, was my own maid.

The marble swung back into place and, as I stared at the now innocent looking fireplace, an even more alarming thought occurred to me. Had Elaine discovered Rosie's secret and died because of what she knew?

My first instinct was to rush to the library to tell Rolf of my discovery. In fact, I was already halfway to the door when another burst of laughter came from within. If he was as befuddled as last time, it would be useless to rely on his help. He would betray his presence in the passage and give Rosie time to escape.

I thought of rousing the servants, but knew that by the time I had awakened them, it would be too late to catch her. The only solution was for me to follow Rosie by myself, learn as much as possible about her con-federates, and then acquaint Rolf with the facts.

She had placed her hand under the mantle to release the door. I copied her action but at first could feel nothing, then my fingers touched a smooth knob. Nothing happened when I twisted it, but a firm push upwards released the mechanism. Once again the seemingly solid marble slab swung open.

It was fortunate I had brought a candle from my boudoir, for the cavity was black. I looked for signs of light from Rosie's candle, but the darkness was absolute. Following her example, I lit mine and stepped through the aperture. What I had thought possibly a ladder was in reality a steep flight of stone steps. I wasted precious seconds seeking the closing knob then, with a pounding heart, I began the descent.

After the first dozen steps there was a sharp right angle bend, then a spiral stairway going down. At the bottom I estimated I was standing some fifteen feet under the house enclosed in a tomb-like hush. Before me was a tunnel so low I was forced to stoop. I walked for what seemed like hours, but was probably less than ten minutes, when the candle flame flickered. The way ahead was blocked by more steps, or rather chunks cut away from the earth. At some time water had dripped down them, so they were now covered with a dangerous slime. I climbed them as best I could, holding the candle in one hand and trying to protect my skirt with the other.

My ears had become so accustomed to the silence and my nerves were so taut, that a drip of water sounded like a drum beat. As I neared the top I heard voices. One was Rosie's, but it was the other which set my heart fluttering, then numbed me. There was no mistaking that modulated, gentle voice. Rosie's tryst was with Howard Layton.

I was bewildered. It was impossible for them to know each other. Howard, for that was how I thought of him, was a casual visitor, sent here to recover from the wounds he had received fighting for England.

Yet, was he? I had only his word for that. I was remembering the sure way he galloped through a dense mist; the speed with which he acquired the cottage; his knowledge of fenland customs; the night at the Dog and Partridge when I had needed assistance and was unable to find him. His arrival in the district had coincided with that of the prisoners. Was that accidental or prearranged?

He was a stranger to me; a forbidden acquaintance. He meant nothing to me, never could.

Though I told myself these facts, I knew they were not the whole truth for, in my heart I still hoped that Rolf would relent and permit me to retain his friendship.

My ears strained to catch the gist of their conversation. It was impossible to hear more than an occasional word, but that was all I needed, to know how right Rolf was in protecting me from him. They were discussing tides. Rosie suggested that two nights hence might be the best for the crossing. Any hope I had that the assignation might have an innocent explanation vanished. There could be no doubt that they were planning the prisoners' escape.

My duty was clear enough, I ought to find Rolf and acquaint him with the facts and identity of the traitors.

Could I do it? Could I be the one responsible for their lawful suffering? Death for treason was likely to be painful. How could I cause such misery to the girl I looked upon as a friend and the man who had saved my life?

Rolf would consider it their just reward, but he did not know them as I did. Both had shown me many kindnesses. Yet it was my duty to report them, otherwise I too would be guilty of treason. Why had I not stayed in my room as Rosie asked? I could have slept peacefully with none of this torment tearing me two ways.

I was standing on the top step. Behind me the trap lid rested against the wall, in front was a rotting door. I did not need to see the rat-eaten bed, the dirt and cobwebs, to tell me where I was. Long ago I guessed the passage's destination. It was the only explanation for the gamekeeper seeing a non-existent ghost at the cottage. It was a perfect escape route for anyone trapped in Marsh House. What had once been the refuge of Royalists, was now the haunt of those willing to jeopardize their king and country for a handful of sovereigns.

Sickened by the affair, I descended the steps, knowing that unless I reached the house unseen, my own life would speedily end.

I hastened along at such speed my candle almost went out. Once I thought I heard a noise behind me, but when I peered back into the darkness, I could see nothing. At last I saw the steps circling upwards. It was difficult to hold the support rail, the candle and my skirt. Several times I tripped and almost fell, but at last I was fumbling for the lever. To my relief the marble swung open easily. I was once more in the breakfast room. It looked so peaceful, so ordinary, that tears filled my eyes.

I brushed them aside. This was no time for weakness. With lagging footsteps I crossed to the library, reluctant to set in motion the events which would culminate in Howard's capture. I had opened the door before realizing the significance of the extinguished candles in the anteroom. Rolf and his companions had gone to bed.

Returning to the fireplace I stood staring down into the cavity, then, realizing it would be unwise for Rosie to guess I had discovered her secret, I swung the marble back into place and went upstairs.

My nerves were taut strung. I wanted to crawl into bed, hide my head beneath the clothes, as though by doing so I could eradicate the secret my prying had revealed. Yet this was Rolf's house. He had every right to know what was happening.

As I crossed the balcony towards the west wing, I thought I had reached the bottom of my misery, that nothing could be worse than this moment. Yet fate still had another card to play; a final trick to make me regret even more bitterly my wayward desire to solve mysteries.

I could see from the faint line of light beneath Rolf's door that he had not yet settled for the night and my hand was raised to knock when I heard voices within. One was certainly Rolf's, the other was that of a woman.

'My own dearest,' Rolf was saying, 'how can you doubt my love? Have I not proved it many times? Be

116

patient, my lovely one, my precious sweet. It'll not be for long I promise you.'

Her reply was indistinct, but the tone was wheedling. Even as I hesitated, he spoke again.

'I must marry her and beget an heir. It's the only way I can gain control of the Hawkins fleet. The doltish old fool has willed everything to her, as yet, unconceived son. Once she has that son, my son, she can go to hell for all I care. I'll have controlling interest of the two companies and that's all I'm concerned about. Once I've achieved that, the whole world can learn of our love and you can be the mistress here.'

Again I heard the murmur of her voice and Rolf's answer.

'He's an old man, my darling. His end is nigh, that's why he's eager for the marriage. He knows a woman can't control the business. This is his scheme to preserve it for his heirs. It's a contrivance which suits me admirably, for they'll be my heirs too.'

I know now I should have crept into my room, collected Patch and left the house before any of the servants stirred. I could have gone to the Hall, the servants there would have protected me until Grandpa's return, but few act wisely when as angry as I was at that moment.

Without stopping to consider the consequences, I flung open the door. The woman was sitting up in bed, black ringlets tumbling about her shoulders, her large eyes startled by my sudden appearance. She pulled the silken bedcover up against her, but not before I had seen the soft roundness of her bare breasts. For the second time that night I had lain a ghost. She was the woman I had glimpsed in the mirror.

Rolf was sitting on the side of the bed, still wearing his breeches; his shirt open to the waist. He looked bewitchingly handsome with his hair slightly rumpled and his naked skin dark against the whiteness of his linen.

My final shred of self control snapped. I lunged at him, beating my hands against his exposed chest.

117

'How dare you,' I sobbed, 'I'll never marry you. Never, never, never and you can't make me.'

He caught my wrists: 'How long have you been listening?'

He was hurting my arm, but I was beyond caring.

'Long enough to know you're an adulterous cheat and liar. No decent man would bring his mistress into the room next to where his future wife was sleeping. Grandpa shall hear of this. He'll cancel the agreement.'

'Indeed!' He pushed me and I fell sprawling onto the bed. The woman hastily moved her feet from beneath my weight. 'Then let me remind you of a few facts. You might be his only living kin, but he has not the slightest feeling for you. How can he have? He's met you only once and not come near you since.'

'That's because he doesn't want me to catch smallpox.'

'If you believe that you're a fool. To him you're just a pawn in the bargain. His only interest is that his great-grandchild should inherit both businesses. He'll care not the slightest what becomes of you once the child is born.'

I pulled myself up and faced him. None of my step-mother's taunts had ever made me so irate, for I realized that he possibly spoke the truth. Beyond ordering some clothes for me, Grandpa had not shown the slightest interest in my welfare.

'Neither of you can force me into marriage against my will.'

'Wrong again. Silas Hawkins and I are the two most influential men in Marshsea. No-one flaunts our wishes.'

'Then here's one who will. I'll go away, hide somewhere you'll never find me.'

I spoke hastily and immediately the words were uttered I realized my mistake. Only fools revealed their intentions in such situations. Rolf grasped my arm, twisting it behind my back, so that I could not move without an agonizing pain shooting to my shoulder. He forced me towards the door.

118

'Where are you going?' the woman asked, speaking with a slight lisp.

'To the old nursery. She'll be safe enough there until she regains her senses. You'd better come too. I need someone to carry the light.'

We made an odd trio as Rolf forced me along the corridor and up the servants' staircase. The woman opened the door and Rolf flung me into the room so roughly, I stumbled and fell to the floor. As a key turned in the lock, I rushed to the door, beating against it with my fists, but no-one answered. I looked at the moonlight shining through the barred window. Rolf was taking no chances. I was as much a prisoner as the debtors in Newgate jail.

12

How long I lay on the damp bed, staring at the moonlight, I shall never know. Eventually I fell asleep. When I awoke, sunlight was throwing shadows of the window bars onto the oak furniture, adding a mite of warmth to the freezing room.

I wondered what reason Rosie had been given for my absence and if she would believe it. Even as hope that she might come searching for me rose in my numb body, I realized she would not. She was too involved in her own insidious affairs to concern herself on my account.

I recalled Howard's advice as we dined at the Dog and Partridge. 'Fen tigers are funny folk. Never ask questions. Not if you want to stay out of trouble.'

Yesterday I had been happy in my ignorance. Had I heeded that warning, I would have gone to my wedding next week, if not eagerly, at least willingly, unaware of the unhappiness which awaited me at Marsh House once a son was born. One thing was certain. There would be no child now. If it cost my life, I would wreck Rolf's plans in that direction.

I walked about the room, shaking my arms and legs in an attempt to restore some warmth to them. Outside the birds flitted amongst the trees mockingly free. In the distance the red sails floated over the sparkling sea. Such an ordinary scene, it made my present position seem incredible.

A movement on the lawn attracted my attention and I saw Rosie with Patch running beside her. I rapped at the glass, but she was too far away to hear me.

It was the longest day of my life. There were no books and no clock. Only the sunlight dawdling across the walls distinguished morning from afternoon. When hunger added to my other discomforts, I wondered if Rolf intended to starve me into submission.

The door finally opened at dusk. Mason guarded the opening as Briggs entered with a loaded tray. Perhaps it was a trick of the light, for the room was dim, but I thought his expression was one of pity.

'Your dinner, madam,' he said, placing the tray beside me.

His presence gave me the first glimmer of hope that I might still have a friend. I glanced at Mason wondering if I dare make a dash for freedom, but it was obvious from his wary stance that I would have no hope of passing him. So instead I asked for a fire to be lit and candles brought.

'The cold in here is perishing,' I said. 'Unless I have some warmth I shall freeze to death.'

'I'll speak to the master,' Mason said, indicating to Briggs to vacate the room.

As the door closed I looked at the tray. There was some soup, a little chicken with vegetables and some of cook's apple pie. My first instinct was to refuse to eat anything until I was released, but my hunger was too great. Besides, abstinence would harm no-one but myself. It would be more sensible to accept everything I was offered, lull them into thinking I was subdued, until I could escape.

It was dark when I finished eating, for the moon had

not yet risen, and I realized I was at the beginning of another long, cold night. Like a blind person I groped my way to the bed and huddled beneath the covers for warmth.

A long time later Mason returned with a candle. Briggs was carrying a basket of wood and though I know it sounds foolish, I could have hugged them both, so pleased was I by the thought of having a little comfort.

Briggs worked in silence, adding more wood as the flames rose. I prayed they would not leave until the fire was established.

Throughout the operation Mason remained like a jailor beside the door, his eyes watching me as though anticipating an escape attempt. I was indeed tempted, but both men were strong. I would be overpowered instantly and probably left without even the comfort of a fire.

When the task was completed Mason indicated the tray. Briggs carried it out and once more I was alone.

As I crouched by the increasing heat I began shaking like a person with ague, then as my body thawed, the trembling ceased. I was gladdened by the pile of wood lying on the hearth. There was enough to keep the fire burning until morning. Mason had taken away the candle, but there was sufficient firelight to see about the room. Soon I was warm enough to discard my coat. I pulled the rocking chair nearer the blaze and eventually fell asleep.

I awoke suddenly, my senses alert. Noticing the fire was low, I was leaning down to add another log, when a metallic noise attracted my attention. As I watched, the door opened. For a moment the man stood in the opening, then with a swift stride, he crossed to me. I thought it must be some kind of hallucination, some trick of the firelight, or that I had not yet awakened from my sleep, but his arms were real enough as they closed about me.

'Henrietta, are you all right, my darling, my precious sweet? Have they harmed you?'

'Howard! I don't understand . . .'

His emotions at that moment were too great to be controlled. His lips crushed upon mine, preventing

121

questions. I was too bewildered; too unprepared to resist. Forgetful of all else, I relaxed in the ecstasy of that unstemmed flow of love. Howard was holding me. We were exchanging kiss for kiss, our lips meeting in a blissful union. What he had done, why he was here, was not important. I forgot he was a traitor; that it was my duty to denounce him. All I knew at that moment was that I loved him as I had never thought to love any man. He was crushing me against himself; kissing me as I longed to kiss him. Nothing mattered but our love. Whatever happened later, I would always have the memory of this spontaneous moment; this magical rapture. My blood pulsated as I clung to him.

Rosie's voice reminded us of the need for action. She was standing in the doorway candle in hand.

'You must hurry,' she said, crossing to where my coat lay on the bed. 'Put this about you and come at once.'

Howard released me. I could feel that his reluctance was as great as mine.

'Rosie's right. We must make good your escape.'

'But I don't understand . . .'

'There's no time for questions. Can you manage to walk?'

Rosie was urging us towards the door. 'Keep quiet as possible and follow me,' she whispered.

I was too dazed by the suddenness of events to argue. All I could think of was freedom. Lovely, glorious freedom. That and the knowledge that Howard loved me. It was not until we had reached the bottom of the servants' staircase that I remembered Patch.

'I must get him,' I said, turning to run up to my boudoir, where I expected he would be. 'I can't leave him behind.'

Howard gripped my arm and forced me on.

'He's already safe. Rosie saw to that this morning.'

We passed through the servants' door into the vestibule. At the entrance to the secret passage Rosie thrust the candleholder into Howard's hand.

'You take it. I'll manage with this,' she said, taking one from a sconce. 'I'll replace it in the morning.'

'Aren't you coming with us?' I asked.

'No. They mustn't guess I helped you to escape.'

'Are you sure you'll be safe?' Howard asked.

I was surprised by the concern in his voice.

'Yes, providing I behave as normal.'

There were many questions I wanted to ask but Howard was already descending the spiral staircase, candle in hand. As I followed him Rosie swung the marble back into place and we were alone. I attempted to quiz him but he would say nothing beyond urging me to hurry.

'We must reach safety before daybreak,' he said.

The moon was shining through the broken shutters as we stepped from the cupboard. Howard extinguished the candle and hid it amongst the dirty crockery. He opened the outside door cautiously, then, having assured himself that no-one was watching, he took my arm and guided me through the wood. We walked so quickly conversation was impossible. Instead of using the road he guided me across the fields, finding the hedge gaps and dyke crossings with the skill of one accustomed to the journey. It reminded me of his connection with the enemy.

The knowledge gnawed. Traitors were cruel men who would sell their souls for money. They were not gentle and considerate, as kind and loving as Howard. Yet, in my heart I knew it was the traitor's very ordinariness which prevented his discovery. My predicament was unbearable. It was my duty to report what I knew, but how could I do it now? Yet if I remained silent I would also be guilty.

At the outskirts of Marshsea we heard a sentry challenge a lone coach.

'They're wasting their time tonight,' Howard muttered, and I knew he was thinking of the planned escape.

I should have called to the sentry, told him the traitor he was seeking was beside me, assisting my escape from Marsh House. Instead I remained silent, unable to betray the man I loved. Yet, had I but done my duty, a great deal of my subsequent misery would have been averted. As it was, I quietly followed Howard through the shadows to a cottage on the opposite side of the harbour to his own.

He knocked twice, paused and knocked again. Immediately the door was opened and I was urged into a shadowy room which was lit only by fire-light.

'You got her then?'

The man's voice was coarse and had the long vowels. A candle flamed into life as he held it to the fire.

The small room was sparsely furnished. Besides the settle, there was a table, three wooden chairs, a bed and some shelves on which stood some cooking and eating utensils.

The man was a good three inches taller than Howard and exceedingly broad. He wore black serge trousers and a woollen jumper. I wondered where I had seen him before. At first I thought he was one of the men on the beach the morning I rescued Patch, then, as the candle-light caught his gold ear-rings, I remembered him. He was the giant who had called the landlord on our arrival at the tavern. Yet he had given no sign then of knowing Howard.

I was about to demand an explanation when something soft flung itself against my leg. Patch was at my feet, his stumpy tail wagging joyously, his black eyes sparkling a welcome. I lifted his wriggling body into my arms and was rewarded with the feel of his warm tongue on my face.

'Rosie smuggled him to me and I brought him here this afternoon,' Howard said. 'He was a little frightened at first, but he'll be content now you've arrived. This is Captain Peacock. He's the skipper of your grandfather's "Sally Jane". His brig's due to sail in an hour, but you'll be safe enough in his cottage until your grandfather returns. No-one'll think of searching for you here. Not even Rosie knows where I've brought you.'

It was obvious from the Captain's clumsy bow that social niceties were rarely part of his life. He was more at home lifting the smoke blackened kettle from its hook over the fire and making a hot toddy for each of us.

Howard helped me from my coat and then seated himself beside me on the settle. As we sipped our warming drinks he began answering my questions, starting with an apology for deceiving me about his name.

'Oh yes, I'm a major right enough,' he added. 'Major Middleton-Brown.'

He paused as though expecting me to recognize the name.

'Does it mean nothing to you?'

I thought hard. There had been so many battles during the past few years. Yet I could not remember hearing it in connection with any of them. As I shook my head, he continued:

'Have you not heard of Elaine Middleton-Brown?'

'Rolf's first wife? I've not heard her maiden name before.'

'She was my twin sister.'

'Then you know Rolf.'

'No. I was fighting overseas when she married, but she seemed happy enough, though it was an arranged marriage. Her letters continually praised him. It was only gradually I realized something was frightening her. I wanted to return to England to discover the cause of her fear, but I couldn't get leave of absence. For a long time I received no news. The next letter to reach me was from Rosie telling me of Elaine's accidental death. It was a dreadful shock. She had been dead four months before I knew of it. I threw myself into the fiercest battles. I wanted to forget I had not been near to help her when she needed me. I took so many risks a legend arose that I was indestructible.

He smiled ruefully and I noticed the laughter lines around his eyes.

'Truth to tell, I began believing it myself. Then a bullet in the chest ended my activities. Everyone prophesied my death. In fact, one blundering fool of a subordinate wrote to my family commiserating with them on my demise. Fortunately he was premature. I survived the voyage to England and thanks to my mother's devoted care, I recovered. Rosie heard of my wound and wrote to sympathize. She grew up with us, you know.'

I nodded. 'She told me her mother worked for your family.'

'It was from her that I heard about Elaine's hallu- cinations. Like Rosie I was puzzled. My sister was the most sensible of people and certainly not fey. If she said she saw or heard something, you could depend upon it that she did. When I learned of the mystery surrounding her death, I decided to do some investigating of my own. I'd intended to wait for the summer, but when Rosie told me that Cheval was marrying again, I decided to come at once. As Rosie was already working in the house, we decided I might learn different opinions about the accident if no-one knew of my connections with Elaine. Hence the false name. Cheval and I had never met, so there was little chance of my being recognized. I had not bargained on meeting the new bride and falling in love with her.'

His tone was matter of fact, but the words sent my heart racing with happiness. For a moment all I could think of was his admission of love for me. It was difficult to concentrate as he continued:

'One of the worst moments of my life was when I heard you were living at Marsh House, for I had thought you safe at the Hall.'

'But why did you suspect I might be in danger?'

'We knew that if Elaine were murdered, and we were becoming increasingly sure that she was, it was probably something to do with the people she said she saw in the house at night. What we have not yet discovered is how much, if anything, Cheval knows about these happenings. I told Rosie to lock your boudoir door. We didn't want you stumbling upon the secret which was probably responsible for Elaine's death. Unfortunately, we had not reckoned with your curiosity.'

'Anyone discovering their door locked at night would become curious.'

'Most young ladies would be too frightened to go to such lengths as you did to discover the cause.'

Excitement pulsated through me. Howard was making his part in the mystery sound so plausible.

'Have you discovered it? Marsh House's secret, I mean?'

'Our luck was no better than yours. We know there's

a woman who visits Marsh House and who is able to come and go at will.'

'Through the secret passage, you mean. So Rolf does know of its existence. I wondered if he might. Mrs. Dobbs said that as a child he used to vanish without trace.'

'Steady there. You're jumping the firing line. She appears to be able to come and go without using the passage.'

'I don't understand.'

The Captain leaned forward to offer Howard some tobacco. After obtaining my permission, Howard accepted the pouch and pushed his pipe into it. Patch opened one eye to see the cause of the movement and went back to sleep.

'That's the difficulty,' Howard said, lighting his pipe. 'Neither do we. One night Rosie had arranged to meet me at the cottage. As she was coming downstairs after locking your door, she caught a glimpse of a woman entering the breakfast room. Not wanting to be seen herself, she hid in the vestibule. When an hour passed and the woman had not emerged, Rosie decided to take another peep at her. To her surprise the breakfast room and library were empty.'

I frowned, unable to understand why Howard was making so much of a simple matter.

'It's as I said,' I retorted. 'She left by the passage.'

'No, that's just what she didn't do. You see, Rosie waited a little longer, then decided to come along the passage to join me. She felt sure that by then I would have met the lady anyway, but, true as I sit here, Rosie was the only person to step from the passage that night.'

For a moment I was silent, at last appreciating the significance of Howard's statement.

'Mayhap you fell asleep and missed seeing her.'

'In that cottage! There's not even a chair to sit on.'

'Then what are you suggesting? That she's a ghost or that there are two passages?'

Howard studied the carved figure on the end of his pipe.

'Secret passages are expensive to build so only a

127

madman would construct two, even in Cromwell's days.'

'She's not a ghost,' I replied. 'Not if it's the woman I saw. She was certainly of this world.'

'If only we knew who she is or what she's doing at Marsh House.'

'The answer's obvious. She's Rolf's mistress.'

'I wonder if you're right.'

'I know I am,' I replied, and told him how I had discovered her in Rolf's room last night.

'It's a damned odd thing to do,' Howard puffed thoughtfully at his pipe. 'Why should he have her in his room while you're in the house? He could easily house her in the town and you'd be none the wiser.'

Until that moment I had been too angry with Rolf to view the matter clearly. Now I realized Howard was right. It was a stupid action and yet Rolf was adroit. Not the type to take risks without good cause.

'There's another thing,' I added, telling him of my tour of the house. 'None of the rooms is being used by a woman. I was particularly looking for signs of that.'

'If she's not living at Marsh House she must be living nearby, so why doesn't Rolf visit her there? Also Rosie swears there's no stranger in town. In such a small place everyone knows everyone else. They're quick to notice outsiders.'

I smiled at Howard. 'You'll soon have me believing I imagined her.'

I intended it for a jest, but his face remained serious as he said: 'Elaine sees her and dies; you see her and are locked away.'

'Only because I refused to marry him. He intended to force me into it.'

'I don't see how he could do that. Surely your grandfather would prevent it.'

'He said Grandpa would side with him.'

'I doubt that. He wouldn't force you to keep the agreement in such circumstances. He's too just.'

Howard's confidence in Grandpa gave me fresh hope. 'How did you know where to find me?' I asked.

'Briggs told Rosie.'

'Briggs?'

He smiled at my surprise. 'They're sweethearts and hope to leave here and marry when the mystery surrounding Elaine's death is solved. Meanwhile they keep their troth secret. Cheval doesn't approve of his servants marrying. Briggs passes on to us any information he thinks might be useful.'

'Does that include news of the Frenchmen?' I asked, remembering the conversation I had overheard and feeling a sudden joy at the possibility that Rosie might have been merely passing on a message.

Howard looked startled and glanced at Captain Peacock.

'That's a deuced odd question. Why should Frenchmen have a connection with Marsh House?'

Having started the topic I had to continue. I told him how I had witnessed his meeting with Rosie.

His laughter was spontaneous, yet it failed to reach his eyes. 'Gad. Would you hang me by such flimsy evidence? Didn't anyone tell you never to eavesdrop? We merely discussed which was the most likely night for them to cross. That's the main topic in Marshsea. Every man, woman and child has talked about it during these last few days.'

'Then you're not in league with them?'

'Do you really consider me capable of such evil?'

He moved closer, his hand stroking my hair. As I turned to look at him our lips met. For a moment I forgot the Captain sitting opposite; Patch snoozing by the hearth; the fact that Rolf was not yet aware of my escape.

The Captain spoke. 'It's nigh on time we were going,' he said. 'I'll make some gruel first to keep out the cold.'

'Are you both leaving?'

Howard took my hand in his. 'The Captain's boat is due to sail on the tide and I must not be seen near this cottage. You'll be safe here until your grandfather returns this evening. No-one'll think to look here for you. I'll come back when darkness returns and take you to the Hall. Meanwhile you must promise not to stir from the cottage nor answer the door should anyone knock.'

After they left I washed the gruel bowls with water from the bucket beneath the table, then followed Howard's advice to try to sleep. Patch, although he knew it was forbidden, jumped onto the bed and snuggled against me. I was so relieved to have him with me again, I hugged him closer and allowed him to stay.

When I awoke the fire was little more than white ash. From the noise and bustle in the harbour, I judged the morning to be well advanced.

I added more wood to the fire and blew life back into the embers. Then I washed and dressed leisurely, knowing there would be little to occupy me until Howard returned.

It was dark in the room, for Howard had warned me against opening the shutters. I lit a candle and prepared some gruel for Patch and myself. When the sparse meal was over, I found a chink in the shutters through which I could watch the harbour activities. The fisherwives pausing to gossip; the children trundling hoops; ships being unloaded. I knew from the flurry of activity that one of Rolf's brigs was preparing to sail.

Across the harbour I could see Howard's cottage and wondered if he too was waiting indoors, or if he was out searching for more clues concerning his sister's death. After such a lapse of time, the chances of discovering any conclusive evidence was nil, yet I could sympathize with his yearning to seek justice for her. If the shooting was intentional, it was only right that the murderer should be caught and punished.

Two soldiers came striding along the quay and stopped at his door. I was pleased for it meant I might see him talking to them. To my intense delight he answered their knock. He was too distant for me to distinguish the expression on his dear face, but I was content to know he was merely across the harbour from me.

Gradually I became aware an argument was developing. Then they entered the cottage. A few minutes later they emerged and walked towards the barracks; Howard between the soldiers.

I spent the remainder of the daylight watching for

130

his return. When darkness fell my anxiety increased. I invented all manner of reasons for the soldiers' visit. Each footstep on the cobbles sent me racing to the shutters to peer out into the darkness, hoping it might be Howard. As they passed the cottage I returned to the fire feeling more depressed. I waited for a long time, hoping against hope that he would come. At last I lifted Patch into my arms and silently left the cottage, knowing I must make my own way to the Hall.

As I stumbled along the cliff road I was glad the moon had not risen, for it made the possibility of my being seen less likely. Although I had made the journey only twice before, once with Howard and once with Rosie, I had taken great interest in the route and was therefore able to find my way. Even so, I was relieved when the iron gates loomed before me. I lifted the latch on the small side gate and stepped into the grounds.

The carriageway was long and the temperature dropping rapidly in preparation for another sharp frost. Although I walked fast, I was shivering when I reached the front door. As usual the maid opened it only a crack and the draught promptly extinguished her candle.

'Who be it?'

'Miss Debnam. Pray open the door that I may enter.'

I expected her to close it while she fetched Mrs. Gawthrop. Instead she unfastened the safety chain.

'Has my grandfather returned from his journey?' I asked, standing Patch on the vestibule floor.

'Yes, Miss.'

'Then tell him I'm here and wish to speak with him.'

'Yes, Miss. Will you please to come this way.'

I was surprised she had not been taught to convey the news of my arrival to her master before ushering me into his presence. However, I remembered Mrs. Gawthrop saying she had not long been in service and dismissed her lack of correct training as being due to the smallpox upheaval.

Not once did it occur to me that my arrival might be expected. Therefore I was completely unprepared for the scene which greeted me as I entered the drawing-

131

room. Seated on one side of the fireplace, a pipe in one hand and a wine glass in the other, was my grandfather, looking every inch the country squire. Confidently relaxing in the opposite chair was Rolf.

13

I was stunned by the sight of Rolf. Throughout the wait at the cottage and the lonely journey, I had believed that I would find sanctuary at the Hall. It had not occurred to me that Rolf might be there. I wondered what explanation he had given for my departure from Marsh House and I knew I must take care to avoid any traps he might bait for me.

'Come in, Henrietta,' he said. 'You've proved me right. I assured your grandsire we need not concern ourselves for your safety. I was positive you would come here fast enough once you learned of your lover's arrest.'

'What do you mean? How do you know he's been arrested?' I asked, remembering the last time I had seen Howard, he was striding along between the two soldiers.

The news coming so soon after the shock of discovering Rolf here, caused me to speak without due care, thus unwittingly corroborating his story. He turned to Grandpa.

'Is that not proof enough of her guilt? What other evidence need you?'

'Guilt of what?' I asked.

Grandpa rose from his chair, his face red with anger. I faced him with a bigger show of courage than I was feeling and for a moment the two of us stared at each other. Patch growled uneasily and moved nearer to my feet.

'I'm waiting for an explanation,' Grandpa said.

'For what? I cannot explain without first learning what I'm supposed to have done.'

'Play not the innocent with me, m'girl. You know well

enough. How dare you play dart and dagger like a camp follower. When I think of the trouble I took to arrange this match for you, it makes me livid that you should show so little gratitude.'

'I've done nothing to deserve your displeasure. It's Mr. Cheval who's the guilty one.'

'Play not the coquette with me, m'girl. He had only to mention a lover for you to know exactly who he meant. Trouble not to deny it. I heard your answer clearly enough.'

The colour raced into my face. Howard and I might not be lovers in the physical sense, but we certainly were in our hearts. Rolf's mention of a lover had naturally sent my thoughts winging to Howard, not because we had reason to be ashamed of our actions, but because of my concern for his safety. I fought back my rising panic.

'You may have heard my answer, but you failed to understand it. I know only one other gentleman in the district besides yourselves and this is Mr. Layton.' Fortunately it was his pseudo name which came to my lips. 'When you mentioned that someone had been arrested I naturally thought of him. However, he's not my lover and never has been.' I saw uncertainty flicker into Grandpa's eyes and knew I must press home my advantage. 'I'll swear to it on the Bible, if you wish me to do so.'

Rolf turned in his chair to obtain a better view of us.

'That's a mere herring. Ask her to swear she was not with him last night.'

'Will you do that?'

I looked from Grandpa to Rolf, who sat sprawling in the chair, the diamond on his right hand glinting in the firelight.

'It's true that I was with Mr. Layton last night, but I was not alone with him except for my escape from Marsh House. The remainder of the time we were chaperoned by Captain Peacock. I don't know what Mr. Cheval's told you, but it's unlikely to be the truth. Did he tell you I was being held prisoner?'

'He told me he was forced to lock you in the nursery

133

to keep you safe from your foolish infatuation, until he could return you into my custody.'

Grandpa's reply astounded me. Rolf was certainly clever. By staying so near the truth, he had removed the impact from my story. His arrogant smile frightened me.

'I was locked in the nursery because I caught him in the act of making love to another woman. I said I would tell you and you'd have the agreement made void.'

Rolf eased his long legs to a more comfortable position. His voice was assured. 'You see, it's as I predicted. She attempts to pass her guilt onto me. You've only to ask yourself if it's feasible that I'd entertain a mistress in my room when my future wife was sleeping next door. You are man of the world enough to know that only an imbecile would do that. Yet, be that as it may, let's concentrate on her activities. By her own admission, on her arrival at Marshsea she is brought to your lodge gates by this scoundrel who declines to meet you. Two days later she was seen to enter his cottage and stay there unchaperoned for several hours. Whether or not that was an innocent action can well be left to your imagination. As if that were not infamous enough, she then had the audacity to entertain him at Marsh House during my absence. Is it any wonder that I decided to lock her up until I could return her into your care?'

On listening to the evidence against me I realized how damning it was. Basically everything Rolf said could be proved. All my actions had been innocent, but who would believe that? Even I was fascinated as he continued:

'Then he has the impertinence to abduct her from my house and hide her we know not where. Ask her to deny that.'

'Well?'

Grandpa's voice was calm and I had the impression he was hoping I could defend myself. I turned to Rolf.

'You cannot possibly know that Mr. Layton helped me to escape. No-one saw me leave.'

'You've admitted it yourself. Besides, your maid gave me all the information I needed.'

I gasped, 'Rosie! I don't believe you. She wouldn't.'

134

'There are ways of acquiring the truth.'

I could scarcely believe my ears. 'You can't mean torture.'

'That's an ugly word. Let's say she realized it was to her advantage to tell us of her part in the escape.'

I turned to Grandpa. 'Now you can hear for yourself the manner of man you wish me to marry.'

'I'm more concerned with your conduct.'

'Mr. Layton and I have done nothing wrong. Our actions were a little foolish, indiscreet even, nothing more I assure you. He's the most honest gentleman. He would never encourage me to do anything I need be ashamed of.'

'Yet you went unchaperoned to his cottage, invited him to Marsh House without permission. I've heard more than sufficient to judge the truth. You can consider yourself highly fortunate that Mr. Cheval's still willing to abide by the marriage agreement. I'll tell you this, m'girl. If he wasn't I'd have cut you off without a groat. You could have starved for all I would have cared.'

'I would rather starve. All he wants is to gain control of your money. Surely you must be aware of that.'

'Guard your tongue.'

'Restrain her not,' Rolf said. 'It's as well for you to learn of her tantrums.'

Rolf took a gold snuff box from his pocket, flicked open the lid and took a pinch of the brown powder. It was a languid, bored movement and so infuriated me that I longed to throw the nearest vase at him.

'I don't have tantrums.'

'You're giving a fine example of one right now,' he said adroitly closing the lid.

Grandpa looked thoughtfully from one to the other of us, then he tugged the bell pull. When Mrs. Gawthrop entered, he said:

'Have the guest room made ready. Miss Henrietta will be staying here tonight.'

'But the smallpox, sir?'

'There've been no new outbreaks, so I think we can safely assume the danger to be past. Besides, it'll be for one night only. Tell William to ride to Parson Grey as fast as may be and inform him I wish to speak with him forthwith. You can also tell the servants that Miss Henrietta's wedding is being brought forward to the morrow, so they'd best see to the preparations for the wedding breakfast.'

'You can't do this,' I said, as the door closed behind her. 'I beg you to think carefully. It's your fleet he's after.'

He touched my hair with surprising gentleness. 'You're overwrought, my dear, and know not what you say. Trust me and the day will come when you'll thank me.'

'How can you say such a thing? He's out to destroy not only me but also any son I might bear—your great-grandson. I overheard him telling that woman so.'

Rolf smiled. 'As you see, sir. She has the gift of imagining women where there are none, as my servants will testify.' He turned to me with a show of false charm. 'Those ghosts are figments of your imagination, my dear. They have no existence in reality. No-one else ever sees them.'

'Elaine did.'

He ignored the contradiction. 'Just to prove I'm not the ogre you imagine, I'll strike a bargain with you. Ours is to be a marriage of convenience and I've never pretended otherwise, though I trust that one day a true fondness will grow between us, but what concerns us at the moment is this Layton scoundrel who has you spellbound.'

'He's not a scoundrel.'

He raised his hand to silence my protest. 'Not that I blame you entirely. From all accounts he's a handsome devil and you're far from the first to be swayed by his charms. Even so, he's nought but a fortune hunter; a mercenary searching for a wealthy wife.'

'He's nothing of the kind. He comes from a wealthy family.'

'And yet he lives in a cottage.' Rolf's smile was tolerant. 'Have it your own way, my dear, though one day you'll realize I'm right. At the moment you are in-fatuated and cannot see clearly. You think yourself in love, no doubt.'

'I do love him and you cannot stop me.'

'If you have such strong feelings for him, then you'll be equally concerned for his safety.'

Rolf was baiting a trap and I was being drawn into it. I could do nothing to save myself. It was like being in quicksand. The more I tried to extricate myself the tighter I was caught.

'Here then is my proposition. At the moment he's being held at the barracks accused of abducting you. I need not remind you of the penalty for such a crime.'

'He was rescuing me. If there's a trial I shall say so.'

'Indeed, and who'll believe such evidence? You're far from being the first heiress to have her head turned by an adventurous scoundrel. The evidence is strong against him. If he's brought to trial he'll be found guilty.'

'You dare not bring him to trial,' I retorted, joyously realizing that, after all, it was I who held the trump card. For a second a look of uncertainty covered his arrogant face. He recovered his poise immediately and was smiling again.

'Indeed? I'm positive both your grandsire and I will be delighted to hear why not.'

I rose to my feet and stood beside him, staring down into his blue-green eyes.

'Because he's your brother-in-law.'

It was a pleasure to watch his bewilderment.

'Come now. What whimsy is this?'

'He's Major Middleton-Brown. Elaine's twin brother. He's here to investigate her murder. Yes, murder,' I added.

My triumph was short lived for he began to laugh. I marvelled at the self control which permitted such humour.

'The deuce he is. That's the best jest I've heard in many a year. So this is the nonsense he's been weaving. Oh, Henrietta, my poor innocent fool. Elaine's brother was killed in the battle of Barrosa. I've seen the letter sent to his parents by a fellow officer.'

'The letter was premature. He wasn't killed, only

137

wounded. Besides, if he's not Elaine's brother, then how is it that he knows so much about the family?'

'Through Rosie, of course. They're in league together.'

'I don't believe it.'

'It's true enough. She admitted giving him the information. He's an outright vagabond. However, it's easy enough to prove which of us is the villain. I'll write to my father-in-law this very evening and ask him to send me the letter and necessary proof. I'll warrant he'll be as eager as I to see justice done to the man who's usurping his dead son's name.'

I turned away unsure what to believe. I had accepted Howard's word gladly, because I wanted to believe in him. Yet Rolf looked so confident. I had read of heiresses falling in love with fortune hunters. Until now I had thought such women incredibly stupid creatures. Yet, was I, as Rolf suggested, equally gullible? The only thing I knew for sure, was that I loved Howard, that he was more important to me than my own happiness. I would do anything rather than see him hurt no matter what crime he had committed. Yet I could not rid myself of the niggling suspicion that Rolf might be right, for I remembered his clandestine meeting and conversation with Rosie.

Rolf was speaking again and it was necessary to force my attention upon his words.

'To return to my proposition. If he's brought to trial he'll surely be hanged, but there's an alternative, although I'm not sure the law would approve of my making such an offer. However, as only the three of us are ever likely to know about it, I consider the law's opinion of no consequence. My terms are simple. Either way you must marry me. The deeds are signed and you must obey your grandsire. However, I've no desire to saddle myself with an unwilling bride, nor am I particularly anxious to become involved in the scandal following Layton's trial. It could do harm to both my business and your grandsire's.'

'That's true enough,' Grandpa agreed.

'So, my dear Henrietta, the choice is yours. Marry me willingly tomorrow morning and I'll give you my word that your lover shall go free. Although naturally, I shall demand that he leaves the district and never returns.'

'And if I don't agree?'

'Then, by God, I'll see you have the front seat at his execution.'

I looked from Rolf to Grandpa and knew that either way I was the loser. Whatever my answer I would be saying goodbye to the man I loved.

'How can I be sure you'll honour your word?'

A dull stain spread over his cheeks, reminding me of the episode in the library. I hoped he would attack me again, so that Grandpa could see the temper of the man he was forcing me to marry. Instead Rolf regained his self-control. His voice was icy as he said:

'The word of a gentleman should be adequate for anyone.'

Grandpa tapped the ash from his pipe.

'No, Cheval, while I doubt you not, I think that in all fairness, she should have something more substantial. A letter addressed to Lieutenant Stubbs saying a mistake has been made. That she was not abducted after all. Give what explanation you please, but I'll take charge of the letter. When the wedding's over, Henrietta shall dispatch it to the Lieutenant herself. If she fails to keep her part of the bargain, then it shall be returned to you.'

So the agreement was reached. As I followed Mrs. Gawthrop to the boudoir she had prepared for me, I tried to find comfort in the knowledge that I had saved Howard's life, as he had once saved mine. Now I must be strong, must blot all thoughts of him from my mind. I must pretend I had not met my true love; the one man above all others with whom I wanted to share the remainder of my life.

Far into the night I wondered if I had done the right thing, and had just fallen into a troubled sleep, when Mrs. Gawthrop bustled into the room.

'Here we are, dearie. A nice cup of chocolate to greet your big day. Come you now. Let me wrap this round your shoulders, there's still a chill in the room.'

She tucked the woollen shawl round me, then placed a silver tray on the bed.

'When you've drunk it, just snuggle down again 'till the fire pulls through. The maids'll bring up your bath and water presently.'

The bath was refreshing and I lingered over it, wishing I could delay the wedding.

Mrs. Dobbs arrived from Marsh House with my wedding dress. She and Mrs. Gawthrop insisted upon sharing the honour of grooming me. Had I been marrying Howard I would have enjoyed their reminiscences of other weddings. As it was, I wished Rosie were attending me. When I inquired for her, I was told that she had left Marsh House the previous afternoon.

'Did you see her leave?' I asked, anxious for her safety.

'Mr. Mason saw her. He said she went off jaunty as you please.'

At five to twelve the chaise took Grandpa and me to the chapel by the south gate. As we approached it, I saw the marble monuments in the misty gloom, like silent spectres witnessing this mockery of a marriage. Though no invitations had been issued, the news had spread and many people were peering through the closed gates in the hope of seeing me. For their benefit I smiled, pretending all was well.

The ceremony was brief, partly because the building was so cold, but mostly because Grandpa was anxious to have the matter settled quickly. Earlier that morning I had overheard him telling the parson there was to be no drawn out blessing after the exchange of vows.

As Rolf placed the ring on my finger I glanced at him but his face was inscrutable. At the end of the ceremony he dutifully kissed me. It was the first time our lips had touched, but it was a kiss as cold as the tombs outside. I was at the start of a loveless life. He would take me to beget heirs and at such times my body would ache for another man; for a happiness I might have known had I not been heir to the Hawkins fortune.

True to his word Grandpa handed the letter to me the moment we stepped from the chapel. I had also been permitted to write Howard a farewell note, explaining that by the time he received it, I would be Mrs. Cheval. It was the hardest letter I have ever written. Everything I said was the opposite to what I wished. I had sat at the escritoire last night with the tears flowing over my cheeks. Today I was dry eyed as the groom galloped away to Marshsea. The ceremony was over; my fate sealed. Even Howard could do nothing to save me this time. For better or worse I was Rolfe's wife, with as little right to plan my own life as Patch had to plan his.

It was a dripping day and I was glad, for the sunshine would be an unbearable mockery. The cold penetrated the thick shawl I wore over my bridal dress and I was relieved to reach the warmth of the vestibule fire.

We looked a strange group reflected in the oak framed mirror as we stood warming ourselves. My own face was almost the colour of arum lilies, except for the dark patches beneath my eyes. Grandpa was hearty, although I detected an anxiety in his manner which I had not previously noticed. I wondered if he was having doubts about the wisdom of forcing me into the marriage. Rolf, suave in white breeches, blue jacket and pink cravat, looked the only serene one amongst us. Captain Lloyd, who had officiated as best man, and Captain Easy were both ill at ease, while the little parson pranced, like a sparrow amongst crumbs, from one person to another, spilling his mead as he moved.

When we were thoroughly warmed Mrs. Gawthrop hustled us into the banqueting hall. Throughout the wedding breakfast my thoughts constantly strayed to Howard. I wondered if he had received my letter and how it was affecting him.

When the meal was over Grandpa helped me into my coat and then enveloped me in his bear-like hug.

'Keep smiling, m'girl,' he whispered. 'Things'll not be so bad as you fear.'

As Rolf and I drove away in the phaeton he stood by the storm door waving goodbye, while the captains, and Mrs. Dobbs with Patch, took their places in the four horse carriage.

I was alone with Rolf for the first time since the night

I discovered him with his mistress and I was at loss for conversation. I expected him to refer to the incident, remind me he wanted me only for the money our son would inherit. Instead he was charming. Not by the slightest hint referring to his victory. Indeed, had I been arriving at Marsh House for the first time and therefore unaware of the intrigues enacted there and not acquainted with Howard, I would doubtless have been a contented creature, completely deceived by Rolf's apparent concern for my comfort and his regrets that no honeymoon had been arranged.

'But this is a matter we can remedy when the weather's more suitable,' he said. 'One of the brigs shall be cleaned and we'll sail to London, or Brighthelmsea, if that pleases you better.'

As we passed through Marshsea, the townsfolk were going about their business as though nothing momentous had occurred. I glanced at the harbour, wondering if Howard was in his cottage.

Soon we were negotiating the carriageway to Marsh House. The one place I had hoped never to see again. As always the door opened before the carriage stopped and Briggs came running down the steps to greet us. Rolf assisted me to alight then, to my astonishment, lifted me into his arms and carried me into the house.

In the vestibule the servants were waiting to welcome us with Mason at the head of the line. I was deeply touched when Mrs. Dobbs, who had somehow contrived to reach the house before us, handed me a posy of jasmine.

'With our deepest respects and good wishes for your happiness,' she said.

Everyone was there, indoor and outdoor staff alike. Everyone except Rosie.

'I expect you'll wish to tidy yourself, my dear,' Rolf said, as the servants dispersed. 'I'll wait in the library.'

My heart was heavy as I traversed the stairs. This great house was now my home. Yet how gladly I would have exchanged the grandeur for the tiny cottage by the harbour wall.

A young maid was standing by the open door to Rolf's room.

'Who are you?' I asked.

'Matilda, madam. Mrs. Dobbs said I was to attend you.'

She stood aside obviously expecting me to enter.

'Am I not to have my old room?'

'No, madam. Your things have been moved into here.'

I should have realized that Rolf would expect me to share his bed, yet, until that moment, I had given little thought to the physical side of our marriage. Now it was inescapable.

I glanced round the room I had glimpsed so briefly the other night. It was larger than mine and had small dressing-rooms opening off each side. In one Rolf's silver toilet articles were lying ready for use. Mine were already on the pink frilled toilet table in the other. I opened the closet door and saw my dresses hanging on the hooks.

I returned to the bedroom with its large canopied bed surrounded by blue damask curtains and was vividly reminded of the previous occupant. Tonight I would be sleeping in the bed where he had made love to his mistress. The thought sickened me. I wanted to run into the corridor, to put a great distance between myself and this mocking bridal chamber.

Then, as I looked at the peach coloured coverlet I had last seen draped about her, my tension eased. I realized that having my belongings moved into this room was possibly Rolf's way of saying that such an episode would not be repeated. In future his mistress would not be brought to the house. I wondered if I had misjudged him. Perhaps after all he wanted our marriage to succeed.

Yet it was difficult to reconcile that thought with the conversation I had overheard. Unless . . . was it possible it was his mistress and not me who was being fobbed off with false promises? She had certainly been wheedling.

The more I thought of the matter the more likely it appeared. Since the wedding he had been charming, making things easy for me, even allowing me to come up here alone to accustom myself to the idea of sharing his room. It was as if he regretted his outrageous action against me.

'Do you wish to change your dress, madam?'

Matilda was standing by the door looking awed by the importance of her new position. Glad of the excuse for delaying my return downstairs I acquiesced.

14

During dinner that evening we discussed the proposed voyage to Brighthelmsea. Though I pretended pleasure, I had little heart for the undertaking and I noticed that Rolf too was absent minded. I was relieved when Mason carried in the brandy and I was able to excuse myself.

Normally I went to my boudoir, but tonight that meant going to Rolf's room and I had no desire to await him there. I entered the breakfast room and stood looking at the marble fireplace, remembering this was the night Rosie had suggested for the crossing. Pushing such thoughts from my mind I moved to the library and selected a book of Milton's poems, but it was impossible to concentrate.

Restlessly I mounted the stairs to fetch a shawl for my shoulders. The candles threw pools of light onto the balcony, leaving between them patches of darkness. I thought how lucky the cottagers were, for they had only small areas to light. Not for them the half-lit corridors where robbers or ghosts could hide with equal ease. I told myself to stop being foolish. No-one was in the house but ourselves and the servants. Yet I could not rid myself of the feeling I was being watched. I glanced down at the dim vestibule and thought I saw something move. I almost laughed as Briggs crossed a pool of candlelight on his way to the kitchen. I continued up the stairs, along the balcony and opened the door to the west wing. It was even darker here.

Inside Rolf's room the fire burned brightly, throwing a red glow over the Chinese wall paper. I wished Patch was here to greet me, but his days of sharing my boudoir were over. In future he must sleep in the kitchen.

I lit the candles with a taper from the fire and took one to light my dressing-room. The Paisley shawl was in the second drawer I searched. I tossed it about my shoulders, returned to the master room and was about to extinguish the candles when I heard someone at the door.

'Is that you, Rolf?' I asked, surprised that he should enter so stealthily.

The door was thrown back and Howard stood in the opening. Before I had chance to express my bewilderment he crossed towards me and covered my mouth with his hand.

'For Lord's sake remain quiet.'

He gave me a moment to recover from the shock of seeing him, then released me and closed the door.

'Why are you here? Rolf'll be furious if he finds you. I gave my word never to see you again.'

Never in my wildest dreams had I visualized Howard using the secret passage a second time. My letter had made it abundantly clear that I was now another man's wife.

'To learn more of this nonsense concerning your marriage. I understood it would not take place for another week,' he said.

'This week, next week. What's the difference?'

'Plenty can happen in a week. Why didn't you do as I told you and stay safely hidden at the cottage?'

'Please go before you're discovered. Rolf has a violent temper. I dread to think what he'll do if he finds you here.'

'Not without you. This is a false marriage as well you know. I'll not stand by and see you wreck your life. He's already killed one woman.'

'You can't prove that.'

'Not in law perhaps, but he shot her right enough. The secret passage proves it. Cheval knew she often hid

145

in the cottage during the shoot. It was easy enough for him to reach her via the passage and return to the house unseen.'

'So that was the meaning of the note we found.'

Howard nodded. 'I left it there for Rosie. You see, Captain Peacock was in the woods at the time of the shoot searching for his missing daughter. He saw Mason carry Elaine from the cottage and place her against the tree.'

'Why didn't he mention it at the time?'

'Like Rosie and I, he had no proof. It was his word against Mason's. Besides, he was a trespasser and had no right to be in the wood.'

'I still can't see how that involves Rolf. If she were murdered, then surely Mason is a more likely suspect.'

'He carried no gun.'

'Then why carry her from the cottage?'

'The reason's obvious. He was trying to protect Cheval. An accident couldn't happen in there, it had to be out in the wood. Whether he was an accomplice, knowing in advance a murder was planned, or whether he was acting spontaneously, is difficult to say. Either way his action prevented the truth being discovered.'

'What possible motive could Rolf have?'

'Like you, she was too inquisitive. My surmise is that she accused him of being a traitor and it became a question of his life or hers. Now hurry, we must leave here while there's still time.'

'I'm not going,' I said, realizing that it meant certain death for Howard if he were caught here. 'I'm Rolf's wife now. I went to my wedding quite freely.'

'That can't be true.'

The pain in his eyes made my heart ache. I knew that he was longing for me, just as I longed for him, but I had pledged my word to Rolf. The very fact that Howard was here, a free man, was proof that he had kept his share of the bargain. Now I must keep mine.

'It most certainly is. I . . . I love Rolf, so there's nothing more to say.'

Forcing the lie to my lips was like swearing away my

soul, but somehow I had to persuade Howard to leave. If Rolf discovered him here, there would be nothing I could do to protect him from the gibbet.

He looked astounded. 'I don't believe it.'

Tears were near my eyes. Unless he went quickly I would betray myself. I fought to keep the tremor from my voice.

'It's of no account what you believe. The only matter of importance is that you're trespassing in my husband's house. If you don't go immediately I'll call the servants.'

For a moment longer he stared, then he moved towards me. I thought he intended to hit me and braced myself for the blow. Instead he crushed me in his arms, pressing his lips against mine in such a passionate embrace I could neither breathe nor move. Against my will I was answering his kisses as we clung together in the firelight. When he released me we were both shaken by the force of our emotion.

'You're a bad liar. Come with me before it's too late.'

'Too late for what, may I ask?'

We spun round. Neither of us had noticed Rolf enter. Despite the pistol pointing at him, Howard moved towards Rolf and would, I think, have attacked, had not the captains and Mason entered from the shadowy corridor. Without stopping to consider the consequences, I pushed between Howard and the pistol.

'Shoot me if you must but not Mr. Layton. It's my fault he's here.'

'That much is obvious,' Rolf retorted, 'but as you well know, there can be no bullet for you. At least not yet. You can't die until I have a son. Your lover, however, is not so handicapped.'

Howard's next movement took us all by surprise and nearly succeeded by its very speed. In what appeared one gesture he thrust me aside and was grappling with Rolf, attempting to force the pistol from his hand. It was a hopeless, crazy attempt to save us both and I loved him for it, but it was doomed to failure. Against one man there might have been a fighting chance, against four it was impossible. Howard fell to the floor, knocked unconscious by Captain Lloyd.

I saw Rolf raise his arm and prepare to fire at Howard's defenceless body. I flung myself at the pistol. It fired, but thanks to my action, the aim was inaccurate and the bullet entered the carpet.

Rolf hit me with a blow which sent me staggering against the bed. The blood trickled from where his ring had cut my temple, but the pain was nothing compared to my fear for Howard's life.

'Don't shoot him. Please let him live. I'll do anything you say, anything you ask, if only you'll spare him.'

He turned to me, anger blazing from his narrow eyes.

'You've already proved the worth of your promises: I saved him once on the understanding that you'd be a faithful wife and this is my repayment. You even have the audacity to entertain him here—in my room. By thunder I'll see you whipped to an inch of your life. You'll not forget this night in a hurry.'

'I don't care what you do to me, but please, if you've any mercy in your soul, spare him.'

'He'll have the same mercy as mad dogs.'

Again he raised his pistol. I tried to stop him but Captain Lloyd anticipated my action. He flung me back against the bed and held me fast. I was helpless against his strength. There was nothing I could do to save the man I loved.

Just as I anticipated all was lost, Mason spoke.

'Wait. Don't fire.'

For a joyous moment I thought of him as our saviour, but his following words shattered the illusion.

'A bullet means murder. It'll not be to our advantage if his shot body's found and his connection with Marsh House traced. There's a better way. A man often drowns by accident. Even if his body's washed ashore it will cause little comment, providing it is unmarked by bullets.'

Rolf lowered the gun. 'What do you suggest?' he asked.

'We'll take him with us. It'll be impossible for him

to swim back from our rendezvous tonight. We need only drop him overboard.'

Now I knew for sure that Rosie had indeed been passing on information gleaned at Marsh House that night at the cottage and that Howard was hoping to catch Rolf in the act of helping the Frenchmen. That was why he had said that a week's delay to our marriage would make all the difference.

With sudden clarity I realized how easy it was for Rolf to repatriate the prisoners. His brigs were always coming and going. Who would think of connecting such cumbersome vessels with smuggling? The revenue men would be looking for the smaller, faster ones; the cutters and fishing boats. Yet, once in mid-channel it would be merely a matter of transferring the men to a ship from their own country. I realized too why Rolf had been so against me massaging Captain Easy's shoulder. It was a militia bullet which had caused the injury.

I wondered if Grandpa were also part of this degrading intrigue, but I was inclined to think not. He was highly regarded by the local people, whereas there had been several hints of Rolf's unpopularity, and the impression that folk were biding their time, waiting for him to over reach himself.

Captain Lloyd and Mason carried Howard from the room. I tried to stop them, but Rolf barred the way.

'It's unnecessary to concern yourself on his account. He'll not interfere again, I fancy.'

'Where are you taking him?'

As I tried to force my way into the passage, he again sent me reeling with a stinging blow. Gone now was his charm and I knew that Howard would surely die, not only because he might reveal Rolf for a traitor, but also for a more basic reason. In pleading for Howard's life I had shown the depth of my love for him. Rolf would delight in making me suffer for preferring another man. He would kill Howard as surely as he had killed Elaine, as surely as he would kill me once I had served his purpose. In that instant I knew that Rolf must die.

Pretending to be cowed by the blow I rose slowly to

my feet, my head bowed, my hand clasping my bleeding face. In reality my eyes were fixed on the pistol now held loosely between his fingers. With a quick movement I lunged towards it, desperately trying to turn it upon him, but he was too strong for me and I was flung onto the bed. Then I saw him raise the pistol; point it straight at me.

As I stared at the two sleek barrels I was filled with an anger as great as the hate now directed towards me.

'Shoot if you dare,' I mocked. 'Shoot away the chance of your son inheriting Grandpa's ships. You might get away with murder, but you'll not have Grandpa's wealth. For all your cleverness he has beaten you.'

We stared at each other in the silence of our bridal suite; the strangest bride and groom ever seen. Then slowly, deliberately, he took aim. I lay on the bed like a petrified rabbit, incapable of movement; unable to believe he really intended to kill me. With the fascination of one driven beyond fear, I watched his arm stiffen; saw his finger squeeze the trigger.

The bullet passed so close to my head it pulled at my hair before burying itself into the coverlet. A cynical smile twisted Rolf's lips.

'Perhaps next time you'll think twice before inviting me to shoot. Has no-one told you of my expertise as a duellist? That miss was intentional, but should you be so foolish again, I'll not waste time aiming at your hair. A limb will make a more appropriate target. You can produce the necessary heir equally well with crippled legs. Think on it, my love, and you'll realize the wisdom of co-operation. You brought this on yourself and can expect little mercy. Had you kept to our bargain, life would have been easy for you, as it is . . . but there's work to be done. When tonight's over, my love, I'll have all the time in the world for taming my bride and you will be tamed, make no mistake about that.'

He stepped from the room and locked the door. My head ached, making it difficult to think clearly. There was an increasing stain on my bodice where the blood dripped from the cut on my temple, but this was no time to think of my own discomfort. It was imperative that I obtained help before the brig sailed. Once at sea Howard would indeed be lost. I wiped away the blood and crossed to the window. Unlike the nursery, this one was not barred, but it needed all my strength to lift up the bottom half. Outside the night was black. The moon would not rise for another hour, yet I must raise the alarm immediately. I tried to visualize the front of the house.

The ground floor rooms began at the top of the portico steps and were some ten feet from the ground. The rooms themselves were exceptionally tall, so altogether this window was a good thirty feet up. I could not hope to make a rope that long and to jump would be to invite death or injury.

The portico was outside the original house and did not stretch to the wings, yet some of the ivy which surrounded the pillars had crept along far enough to touch the sill. I leaned out and tugged at a handful of leaves. To my disappointment the tendrils tore from the wall.

I must escape, if not by the window, then by the door. I turned back into the room where the candles were flickering. The door was of oak and would need a solid ram and many men to break it. I wasted several minutes trying to open the lock with a hairpin before returning to the window.

It was then that I had one of those flashes of inspiration which sometimes come if one is desperate enough. The sheets and curtains tied together would not be long enough to reach the ground, but they would have stretched to the portico roof had that been directly beneath me. The ivy tendrils reaching towards this window were too new to take my weight, but if I used the rope to support myself I could probably use the ivy to pull myself towards the portico. It was a dangerous enterprise, but my only chance of saving Howard.

Not daring to contemplate the risk for fear of my courage failing, I knotted the curtains and sheets together and tied one end to the bed post. I pulled against it and to my infinite relief it held firm. I threw the free end out of the window. My heart was thumping as I sat poised between the candlelit room and possible death on the carriageway below.

As I slid from the sill and hung swaying above the abyss, I prayed that I might reach the portico roof without falling. For a while I clung to the sheets not daring to release my grip with one hand. Though the night was below freezing, I was perspiring. I have no idea how long I clung there swaying in the rising breeze, probably little more than a minute, but it felt a lifetime.

Gradually my courage returned. I twisted my left foot round the improvised rope, thus helping to support myself. Then I took a firmer grip with my left hand and cautiously, so that I could instantly regain my grip if necessary, I felt for a piece of firm ivy with my right. Slowly I eased my way downwards and over towards the portico, all the time dreading that someone might come out of the house and see me before I had made good my escape. At long last my fingers touched the stone acroterium. Even so, I decided it prudent to retain my hold on the rope for as long as possible, but I had descended only a yard or so down the column before my foot swung free. From now on I must rely entirely on the ivy. but it grew thickly here and even if I slipped there were but a few yards to fall. When at last I was standing on the steps I almost swooned with relief. My daring plan had succeeded. I was out of the house; free to seek help. Fear for Howard's safety added speed to my feet. Now I had accomplished the perilous descent, I was glad there was no moon, for I was less likely to be seen. I wondered if that was also the reason why the prisoners had waited so long before crossing to France. I wished I knew the path Howard had taken across the fields for it was much shorter and would protect me from unwanted encounters, but I dare not risk searching for it in the dark. By the time I reached the highway I was breathless, but this was no time to rest. The sooner I reached the barracks the more chance there would be of saving Howard.

I thought I heard a movement in the hedgerow and tried to run faster. I had to reach Lieutenant Stubbs before Rolf or one of his servants caught me.

My alarm increased as I became aware of heavy footsteps behind me. The distance was decreasing between us.

'Stop,' a man shouted. 'Stop I bid you.'

Other footsteps joined the chase. I was frantic. I would not get a second chance to save Howard. They were almost at my heels. A hand grabbed me.

'Got this one!'

'Let me go.' I struggled to free myself.

'Who is it?' This second man was better spoken than my captor, and his voice sounded vaguely familiar.

'No telling without a lantern. A woman by the feel of her.'

'Who are you?' a voice asked.

The question created a quandary. Was it wiser to tell my name or remain silent? I wished I could remember where I had heard his voice before.

'Who are you?' I demanded.

'Lieutenant Stubbs. Now your identity, if you please.'

'Oh, thank God.' I was hardly able to believe my good fortune. 'I'm Henrietta Debnam. You must help me.' The words tumbled over themselves as I told of Howard's plight. 'You must save him. Please, please.'

The Lieutenant laughed. 'It seems the Major has overstepped himself this time. I told him to leave well alone, that no woman was worth risking his neck for, but he would know better.'

His reply puzzled me. 'Did you know he was coming here?'

'Naturally. It was thanks to him that we discovered the Frenchies' whereabouts, though it would seem he has a private reason for wishing them caught.'

'If you know where to find them, why are you here?'

'Because this is where they are.'

'In Marsh House, but that's impossible . . .' I stopped, remembering the arrival of the nocturnal carriage, 'but I searched every inch of that house the other day.'

'It's our reckoning there's a secret room somewhere besides the passage. Nicholas Owen often made two hides in a house and the chances are that he did so here.'

'In that case you're ambushing the wrong place. They'll not leave this way, they'll go by the secret passage.'

'The cottage, you mean. That's even better guarded. Either way they'll walk straight into my men.'

'But supposing they shoot Mr. Layton . . . the Major before leaving the house?'

'It's a risk we must take, but I think it unlikely. They have no reason to think their plot unmasked. From your account they intend him to drown, but we shall see they never reach the sea. Anyway the Major would not wish us to wreck the manoeuvre on his account, he's too eager to see the traitors caught. One of my men will escort you to the barracks. You'll be safe enough there until I return. Try not to worry,' he added more gently, 'we'll do our best to protect the Major for you, though I wish he'd left the matter to us.'

It was impossible not to worry, especially when I was seated in the guard room with nothing to occupy my thoughts but the events taking place at Marsh House. One hour passed, then another. A soldier offered me some soup, but I was too worried to touch it. I wished I had some sal volatile for I was fearful of swooning. It was harassing not knowing what was happening outside.

At last the door opened and a young soldier entered. He was hatless and blood stained his tunic.

'We got most of them. Just two still on the run, but we'll have 'em before the night's out,' he said, with satisfaction.

'The Major . . . is he safe?'

He turned to me obviously puzzled by my presence in the guard room.

'Can't say, ma'am. Lieutenant Stubbs'll be along directly. He'll know.'

Another ten minutes passed before the door opened again. Lieutenant Stubbs entered looking pleased with himself, then the room filled with people all talking at once. I saw Mason, his lip cut and one eye rapidly closing; Captain Easy, his arm still in the sling; three strangers who, to judge from their emotional behaviour, were the hunted Frenchmen; Rolf's mistress, bonnetless and hysterical and a Marsh House servant whose name was unknown to me. Neither Rolf nor Howard were amongst the assembly.

'Where's the Major?' I asked, trying to make myself heard above the babble. 'What's happened to him?'

Lieutenant Stubbs took my arm and led me back to the fireside seat. 'Fret not, there's nothing to fear. Cheval and one of his accomplices escaped. The Major and some of my soldiers have gone after them.'

'But he was hurt. Unconscious when I last saw him.'

'Gentlemen of the Major's calibre are tough. Once he learned of Cheval's escape nothing would hold him. He insisted upon joining the hunt; said he had a score to settle.'

The news alarmed me. Howard was thinking of his sister's death. He would be as reckless in his pursuit of Rolf as he was in fighting Boney's army and I could do nothing but sit waiting in this crowded room.

The minutes hovered, each seeming like two. The prisoners were taken in turn to another room for questioning and then locked up for the remainder of the night. Mason tried to implicate me, but fortunately Lieutenant Stubbs was sufficiently acquainted with my role in the affair to prevent my arrest. Even so, I was questioned for almost an hour by his superior officer.

'Let me take you to your grandfather,' the lieutenant suggested, when I returned to the guard room.

'I prefer to stay here. I want to be the first to know when there's some news.'

As we sat by the fire, chaperoned by the soldier writing at his desk, the Lieutenant told me of his life in the Militia but I scarcely heard his words. My ears were straining for the sounds of approaching footsteps.

The watchman called 'Two of the clock and a rising wind', but no-one came. The soldier added more peat to the fire and lit fresh candles. The Lieutenant stopped chatting and we sat listening to the scratch of the quill. The watchman called again. 'Three of the clock on a squally night.'

Lieutenant Stubbs stood up and stretched.

'It's a deuced long night. Why not go to the Hall? You can do nothing sitting here.'

As if to belie his words, the door was flung open admitting a gust of wind and rain. A young soldier entered, his uniform dripping water. His salute was sketchy.

'They got away, sir.'

'The devil they did! How did that happen?'

'They gave us the slip down by the harbour. They managed to board the brig that was about to sail. I tried to get aboard but I was knocked into the water. The sergeant sent me back to change and to give you the news, sir.'

'Where's the Major?' I asked.

'The revenue men joined us. He's gone to give chase.'

'Out on the sea in this gale!' I was horrified.

I did not wait for his reply. Though I had not even a shawl to protect me, I ran towards the quay and joined the huddle of people round the lanterns at the harbour mouth. The Lieutenant followed me and placed a uniform jacket about my shoulders. Like blind people we stared out into the darkness, seeing nothing; hearing nothing but the crashing waves and the wind's roar as it tore at our bodies. The spray stung our faces and soaked our clothes. Standing there I realized how helpless the wives must feel each time the fishing fleet was caught in a gale.

After a long time the rain ceased and the moon gleamed from between the storm clouds. The wind still lunged at us, as though trying to push us into the ravenous sea. The waves were high as a ship's mast. I wondered how any boat could survive against such mighty strength. Once I thought I sighted the brig's sails, but there was no sign of a second boat.

'They're being driven towards the graveyard,' said a bystander. 'Them sands'll get 'em, cripple me sides if it won't. Nought but fools would put out a night like this.'

Fools or desperate men, I thought, and wished there was some way of knowing what was happening out there.

'Can you see the cutter?' I asked.

'Not with this sea. They shouldn't have gone. There's not a hope in hell of catching the devils, 'less it be on the graveyard. Them sands aren't particular who they swallow.'

'Come away, Miss Debnam,' Lieutenant Stubbs was touching my arm. 'This is no place for you.'

'I must stay . . . must know what's happening.'

'It'll be hours before there's any news. You're shivering and the moon's gone again now. You can see nothing here.'

'I must stay.'

'That'll be foolish. You'll catch pneumonia and that'll help no-one.'

I knew he was right, but even so another hour passed before I allowed him to escort me back to the barracks.

The remainder of the night is hazy. I dozed a little sitting in the chair, but always the dreams were filled with pictures of the sea playing cup and ball with Howard's small boat. Several times I dreamed he was on the sandbank and awoke perspiring with fear. At dawn I insisted upon returning to the harbour and was rewarded by the sight of the cutter fighting its way back to the shore.

The group of watchers was smaller now.

'What happened to the brig? Did it get away?' I asked.

The man beside me stroked his grey beard. 'Depends how you look at it. Them sands were 'ungry last night. That be another good ship gone.'

'What of the men aboard? Were they saved?'

'I doubt it. That be something we shan't know till the cutter gets back . . . if she gets back.'

'You mean it's still in danger?'

'There's always danger on a sea like this. Only a fool chances his arm.'

I watched the small boat being tossed by the waves and wondered how anyone on board could avoid being swept into the sea. My fear increased each time it sank

157

into a trough and disappeared from view. I held my breath until it appeared once more. By the time it eventually reached the harbour my nerves were in shreds.

As Howard stepped ashore I flung myself into his arms, oblivious of the onlookers, in my joyous relief of having him near me once more. Then, remembering my husband, I drew away from him.

'Where's Rolf? Is he safe?'

Howard shook his head.

'There was nothing we could do. Not in seas like this. Perhaps it's for the best. A traitor's trial is an ugly affair. Painful to the guilty and their families alike.'

I looked up at Howard; at the salt clinging to his eyebrows and hair; at the weariness of his face and knew he spoke true. This was the best way. The way Rolf would have preferred it. Had he been saved, the future would have held nothing but shame and disgrace and finally a painful death on the gibbet.

Three months have passed since that night. Today the sun is shining as Howard and I drive towards London where I am to meet his parents. As we pass through the villages, they are decorated with Mayday garlands and the young folk are dancing to the pipes and tabors, the winter hardships forgotten in this joyous welcome to summer.

The trial was all the talk for a while, but already it is becoming history. The Frenchmen were returned to Norman's Cross and the law made certain that Mason and his associates will never again betray their country.

Lieutenant Stubbs was right about there being a second hide-away, though it took many days searching to find it. Perhaps we might never have succeeded had not Patch insisted upon sniffing at a certain section of the wall, whenever our quest took us into the secret passage. Even after our attention was thus directed to the spot, it took several more hours before the false wall swung aside to reveal a tiny, but cosily furnished room, where several people could hide for days if necessary. It was well placed, for anyone having discovered the passage would instinctively go on towards the cottage, without realizing their quarry was snug in this extra hiding place.

Since his death I have learned that Rolf married Elaine so that her large dowry might save his business. He had been brought to the verge of ruin by the high winds at the turn of the century, which drove his fleet onto the sandbanks. When he needed more money Mason had introduced him to the profitable trade of smuggling prisoners out of the country.

Now Patch is asleep on the seat opposite to Howard and me. Outside, next to the driver, are Rosie and Briggs. They were married last week in Grandpa's little chapel. It was a happy wedding, with the servants from both houses there to wish them well, and the sun twinkling through the gothic windows. I was glad there was little to remind me of the miserable day when I had stood at the altar. For their honeymoon they are travelling to London with us. Rosie to maid me and Briggs as valet to Howard.

Our wedding will not be for several months yet. Not until the leaves are golden on the trees and the fields freshly ploughed.

Howard will have left the army by then and we will settle at Marshsea, where he is to control the fleet until we have a son old enough to command his own inheritance, and combine the two fleets under the one flag.

There is just one puzzle which remains unsolved. I had always considered it strange that an astute business man like Grandpa should agree to a marriage contract for me, which was apparently so disadvantageous to himself. Now, I realize only too well the contract had said *my* son. There was nothing to stipulate Rolf must be the father, but the fact that I was to be the sole heir if Rolf died without issue, was clear enough.

I saw the look of satisfaction on Grandpa's face as the clause was read out and wondered if he had been aware all along of Rolf's part in the escapes. He would know the penalty for such activities was death. Was it therefore his intention to assist in Rolf's downfall once my marriage had taken place? Could that be the reason for his insistence upon the hasty ceremony and the whispered words 'things'll not be as bad as you fear'?

I wish I knew for sure.

As Howard had warned me on my first night at Marshsea. The ways of the fen folk are strange and a wise person asks no questions.